Decisions

or

Suicide and the other Side

J. K. Proudlock

Order this book online at www.trafford.com
or email orders@trafford.com

Most Trafford titles are also available at major online book retailers.

Note for Librarians: A cataloguing record for this book is available from Library
and Archives Canada at www.collectionscanada.ca/amicus/index-e.html

Printed in Victoria, BC, Canada.

ISBN: 9781-4251-284-3-2 (soft)
ISBN: 9781-4251-284-4-9 (eBook)

*We at Trafford believe that it is the responsibility of us all, as both individuals
and corporations, to make choices that are environmentally and socially sound.
You, in turn, are supporting this responsible conduct each time you purchase a
Trafford book, or make use of our publishing services. To find out how you are
helping, please visit www.trafford.com/responsiblepublishing.html*

*Our mission is to efficiently provide the world's finest, most comprehensive
book publishing service, enabling every author to experience success.
To find out how to publish your book, your way, and have it available
worldwide, visit us online at www.trafford.com*

 **www.trafford.com**

North America & international
toll-free: 1 888 232 4444 (USA & Canada)
phone: 250 383 6864 ♦ fax: 250 383 6804 ♦ email: info@trafford.com

The United Kingdom & Europe
phone: +44 (0)1865 487 395 ♦ local rate: 0845 230 9601
facsimile: +44 (0)1865 481 507 ♦ email: info.uk@trafford.com

10 9 8 7 6 5 4 3 2 1

DECISIONS

TABLE OF CONTENTS

Acknowledgements

This book has been written in stages; each stage was written during that period of healing. Getting to where I am today was not an over the night remedy; many people were involved in my healing, and unfortunately many of these people are no longer a part of my life. Some of these decisions were mine to make and others were the decisions of the people involved.

The book that is before you now has been a work in progress for 13 years; just as the Author has been a work in progress for the same amount of time. Perhaps a new book will emerge from healing that has occurred during the production of this one.

My wife Laurie and our new family are mainly

responsible for the thoughts and healing that has occurred; and for this all to finally be put in a written form that is now called a book. I am so blessed to have found true love in the midst of all the turmoil that I have been through. It was not without a fair bit of trial and error that this finally came about, however I can say that my life has never been as full as it is now. Laurie continues to emulate the meaning of love in our relationship. She goes above and beyond in loving me even in my dark hours. Thank you Laurie for all the love you have shared with me.

My niece Willow Amber-Lynn is one of my Hero's. She has battled so many fights and continues to greet each new day with not only a smile on her face but her ability to put smiles on the faces of all she meets. Thank you Willow for all you have shown me. I wish that you would have been well enough to do the art work on the book cover for me.

My sister Bon and my brother-in-law Loni for their support in getting the me back into me. I lost it for a while, thanks for being patient with me.

Josh Hawley, my web man and artist extraordinaire for all your work. Taking my thoughts and placing them in a picture format, and assisting with getting

DECISIONS

this document into a print ready format. Bless you!

Celia, my long true friend, what a blessing you have been to me and to Laurie. Your notes to Noah inspired me to be a person worthy of such passion and friendship. Thank you!

There are so many more to thank, Pastor's, friends, customers. Thank you all for your input and listening to me as I grew,

DECISIONS

How many decisions do you make a day? Too many to count I would bet; decisions like how to act, feel, and react. So, how do we learn the good decisions from the bad ones? Hopefully we can learn from other people's mistakes, so that we don't make the same ones. Sam Levenson puts it this way **"You must learn from the mistakes of others, you can not possibly live long enough to make them all yourself."** He is one very wise man. I wish I had that wisdom before I went on the journey I am about to share with you. Wisdom, I hope you can gain from reading about decisions I made.

What is the difference between a good decision and a bad decision? A bad decision is one that leads you away from who and what you were destined to be by GOD. Yes GOD! GOD has a plan for each and every one of us. Any decision that we make that causes us to leave His will is a bad decision.

But hold on, if you make a bad decision, can you do anything to change it? **YES!** People have often told me that one bad decision ends it all. <u>NOT TRUE</u> ! The truth is the only really bad decision you can make is the one you make after you find out you have made a bad decision. That decision would be to continue on the road you found yourself on, headed towards yet more bad decisions. So choose to learn! We are all going to make some bad decisions/mistakes. But when we see our mistake, THEN **we** have a choice to make a good decision, a decision to turn around and make things right. Bad decisions however, will still have consequences which **we** must face, but facing them is better than running your whole life and letting one bad decision rule your life. Have you made a bad decision? Take some time as you read this book and reflect on decisions you have made that may be ruling your life now. My prayers are with you as you seek to make good decisions. If you know God, seek Him in your decisions, if you don't know Him, this might be a good time to get to know Him.

This book is about decisions that I made and how they led me to attempting suicide. My prayer in

DECISIONS

writing this book is that even one person will learn from the mistakes that I have made and be able to recover their life before it disappears for them and all those around. Suicide is a bad decision; its affects are felt by so many; family, friends, & the people who find the body and do all the clean up after. Suicide is a **DON'T GO THERE** decision. Read my story. Learn some truths about suicide and life in general.

It is also very important to note that some of what I thought of as truths during my ordeal have turned out to be any thing but the truth. Be sure to read the last Chapter of this book before you make any conclusions about the people and circumstances I have mentioned in this story about my own journey to attempted suicide and back. Thank you!

J. K. Proudlock

DEDICATIONS

This book is dedicated to the few: who stood by me in my recovery; praying for me, loving me even in my darkness. You provided ears to listen, hugs made of gold, and words laced with diamonds from GOD's word, finances at just the right time, words of encouragement and words of reproof. When ever I was on my knees and ready to give into all the battles going on around me, you were there. "**Real friends are those who don't feel like you have done a permanent job when you have made a fool of yourself.**" (out of Krazy quotes for Kids by Vern McClellan) Proverbs 21:17 (NIV) "<u>**As iron sharpens iron, so one man sharpens another.**</u>" Thank you my true friends, for helping me be who I am today! Only God's love and all of your Christ centered love for me, has given me the courage to write this book.

And more importantly, to be all that GOD has predestined me to be. Thank you!

Finally, this book has been written to those whose lives have been forever changed by the awful reality of suicide. May you find God's healing, as you see the comfort He has been to me through my all too real experience with suicide.

1 Corinthians 13:4, 7-8 (NIV) "Love . . . bears all things, believes all things, hopes all things, endures all things. Love never fails." This can only be true when you let Jesus Christ live in your heart, and you live your whole life to be with Him; then and only then can real love, the love that Jesus modeled, be a reality in our lives.

II Corinthians 1: 3, 4 8b - 10 (NIV) "Praise be to the God and Father of our Lord Jesus Christ, the Father of compassion and the God of all comforts, who comforts us in all our troubles, so that we can comfort those in any trouble with the comfort we ourselves have received from God. . . . We were under great pressure, far beyond our ability to endure, so that we despaired even of life. Indeed, in our hearts we felt the sentence of death. But this happened that we might not rely on ourselves but on God, who raises the dead. He has delivered

DECISIONS

us from such a deadly peril, and he will deliver us. On him we have set our hope that he will continue to deliver us." I pray my words will be a comfort to you as Gods' word has been a comfort to me in my time of trial.

The Decision I want to focus on now is to be all that GOD destined me to be as he knit me in my Mothers womb.

J. K. Proudlock

YES I HAD IT ALL
OR DID I?

I remember feeling like I had it all. I was still a newly wed, with a beautiful wife and a brand new daughter. The marriage had its rough spots; being a Father was tough at times but all in all we had fun. I was the leader of youth ministry at our church and there were up to 70 kids in the group; although not once did they all show up for the same meeting. Which in itself was a blessing.

My full time employment was with the City of Calgary as a Telecommunications Specialist. When they don't know what to call you, you are a specialist; nothing special, but a good paying job. Supposedly secure too. I was respected at work, for my knowledge and my quality of work. I had it all.

I had family and friends who I cared about and who cared about me. I wasn't the most popular person around, but that wasn't really important to me. In my mind I had it all.

We had nice furniture, car, truck, camper, big stereo, computer, horses, tack and equipment. A roof over our heads, a comfortable bed, and plenty of food on the table at all times. . I had it all.

I was so involved in everything that seemed to matter, that I missed out on what was really happening. I was losing my identity, my life, my soul. Thou I had gained everything, I had lost everything; until finally I actually lost life itself; my life!

<u>Yes, I had it all</u>, or did I?

SUICIDE

SUICIDE ! ! How does it make you feel? Did your body shut down? Was there a feeling of, I don't want to know about suicide. Was there anger, revulsion, shame, guilt? Or how about this, how could anyone be so weak, so low. What about your friends, family, come on, reach out; get help if you need it, but suicide; no way man, there is no excuse for getting to that point. <u>GROW UP!</u>

SUICIDE ! ! Does it hit you so hard you want to vomit? Do you feel your stomach in the back of your throat, begging to get a real clear shot at the person that was so vulgar as to mention that word; Suicide?

Suicide, does it hit you with its seductive voice; luring you with promises of no more physical or emotional pain; calling out to you when you are hurting, or scared; or how about when you are bleeding and bruised after a fight with a loved one. When you feel so low that all you want to do is remove yourself from this world. **Suicide**, it is such a seducer, a tease, a way out. Can you or have you felt the way it holds you, draws you near. There is a power in her voice that gets under your skin, becomes part of you. Sometimes her voice lies dormant for years, then when we have a break in who we are, **wham**, it hits like a flood. You become consumed by her seductive voice.

SUICIDE, it has a different voice for each of us. But more often than not, you are either on one side of the scale or the other. Repulsed, or seduced. Where are you right now? Do you want to see the other side? I hope so! For those of you who are repulsed by even the word suicide, I hope you will learn just a little tolerance, massive understanding, and the ability to speak the word suicide, with out getting sick to your stomach. For the seduced ones, I pray that you will see that suicide is a voice that calls out in an attempt to get us to do something that is totally against who we were created to be.

DECISIONS

Suicide is one of the devil's ways of feeding us lies about who we are.

SUICIDE, the silent epidemic. Why, because no one wants to talk about it. What will it take for us to wake up to this epidemic that we are in the midst of? AIDS, scares us, cancer, heart disease, MS, drunk drivers, they all scare us. **SUICIDE**, the silent killer. Wake up to its reality. Somewhere in this book, I pray **GOD** will open your eyes and heal your broken heart, and the hearts of those you love.

So, are you ready for a little journey? It may get rough at times. When it does, grab hold of the one thing that will hold you together, **GOD** and his son **JESUS**. Let's go. But first allow me this short prayer. GOD, I pray that you will bring the words out that each person needs to hear and that you would cover the words that they do not need to hear. Give them understanding and peace, as they journey through a portion of my life story. May it speak to each of their lives, no matter where they are on the horrible topic of suicide. I ask this through your son _**JESUS CHRIST**_, who paid for our sins, so that we could have life more abundantly. Amen. There, now we are ready, so let's travel!

13

J. K. Proudlock

Chapter One

B4 it all Began

The topic of my testimony is going to be a hard one for many of you to swallow, let alone understand. But it involves a topic that screams out to be addressed, to be looked at and understood. To be understood as our Father in Heaven understands.

How better to learn about this than to hear a real

life story of someone who has gone through it and learned that GOD and only GOD can heal. So let's begin.

My story while very serious will at times be interspersed with mild humor. I pray this will not offend anyone. So on that note, lets drop right into the toilet and get started.

I received an E-mail message shortly after my return to work and the subject was A Bad Day.

The body of the message follows:

I can not vouch for the authenticity of this piece, but it's good....

Fire Authorities in California found a corpse in a burnt out section of forest whilst assessing the damage done by a forest fire. The deceased male was dressed in a full wetsuit, complete with a dive tank, flippers and face mask. A post mortem examination revealed that the person died not from burns but from massive internal injuries. Dental records provided a positive identification. Investigators then set about determining how a fully clad diver ended up in the middle of a forest fire. It was revealed that, on the day of the fire,

DECISIONS

the person went for a diving trip off the coast - some 20 kilometers away from the forest. The firefighters, seeking to control the fire as quickly as possible, called in a fleet of helicopters with very large buckets. The buckets were dropped into the ocean for rapid filling, then flown to the forest fire and emptied. You guessed it. One minute our diver was making like flipper in the Pacific, the next he was doing the breaststroke in a fire bucket 300m in the air. Apparently, he extinguished exactly 1.7m (5'10") of the fire.

Some days it just doesn't pay to get out of bed!

How true! Some days it just doesn't pay to get out of bed. Especially on days when we get out of bed and leave God at home. Saying, "Okay God, you've been pretty busy lately. You just stay at home today and rest. This will be a no brainer day and I can handle it on my own." Which is what happened to me on August 18th 1995, when in an attempted suicide, I blew myself up.

How can anyone get that low you ask yourself? Let's journey on, and I pray that somewhere during the journey you will find understanding. Understanding of the seductive power of suicide and how it can enter and wreck the perfect plans God has for each of us. But more importantly, I pray that you will gain an understanding of how to arm yourself and those you love to prevent this silent epidemic from affecting your life, a member of your family, a friend, or just someone on the street. My attempted suicide has affected my life, my families, and way too many others, and this is why I tell my story. In the hopes that hearing how GOD has taken this awful thing and given me a new lease on life, will encourage even one person, to reach out and seek GOD as the answer to their pain; as the answer to a friends pain. To prevent the pain I caused some wonderful people in my life from entering the lives of those you care about and who **do care about YOU ! ! !**

For three years prior to my attempted suicide, I had held the position of Director of Youth Ministry at a local Church in Calgary Alberta. I had a beautiful wife and a great bundle of joy in a little 1 year old daughter. Things were going fairly good. Not great, . . . but good enough that I was happy and even though there were many times that I did not show it, I was very much in love with my wife. I still believe that she was a gift to me from GOD; but a gift that I lost due to the bad

DECISIONS

decisions/choices that I made, and the actions that followed those decisions.

I was on my third reunion with GOD and His mercy was so evident in all that He was doing in my life and those around me. He allowed me to witness some incredible miracles. GOD had taken the Youth Group that I was leading and had grown it into 70 youth. It was so wild to see all that GOD was doing. I remember one of the first camping trips that my wife and I took the youth on. GOD was there in such incredible ways. My wife and I were so new to all the wonderful joys and hardships of youth ministry. But I believed so fully in my heart that GOD was there and that He answered prayer for those He had called, especially **The Youth**! I knew beyond a shadow of doubt that something great was going to happen on that trip. But never in my wildest dreams did I imagine the majesty of GOD and His power. You see, GOD provided things before we ever knew that they were needed. And then when they were needed they were right there. Ya right you say. Well, the only way I can think of giving you proof is to share some events that happened.

I thank GOD as I am sure Paul did when he told of the 500 seeing the risen CHRIST at one time. You

J. K. Proudlock

see, most if not all of the people present during these miracles is still alive as they were during Paul's testimony of the risen LORD, JESUS CHRIST.

On Saturday, we went for a hike down a dry river bed. It led to some rock cliffs, where there were rock climbers to watch and talk to. There were hieroglyphics on the rocks and at the very top of the hike; there was a very long but very small graceful waterfall. Sound beautiful? It was! It was a fabulous hike. On the way back, I was kind of hanging back, okay, let's start this book with honesty. It was more like I was so out of shape that I was dragging my butt and pulling up the rear.

The weather looked rather ominous, and one of the group leaders had suggested that if the youth found some good rocks we could collect them and paint them when we got back to camp. This would be an indoor activity used only if the weather continued to get worse, which it sure looked like it was going to. So I asked the youth to look for interesting rocks in the dry river bed.

As we were walking, some of the youth would drop back periodically and talk with me and then race ahead to be back with their friends. On one of

20

DECISIONS

those occasions, I looked down and saw a rock that was broken in half lying with so many others in that very dry river bed. It was symmetrical in shape, but it had been broken at what appeared to be the middle of the rock at a slight angle. Nice and flat, a perfect paper weight for one of the youth to paint a nice mountain scene on for one of their parents. I quickly imagined how it would look set on its angular base, leaning back just a bit with its curved surface displaying a painted scene. It would be so incredibly great, some lucky parent. So I picked it up and hiked on, talking and listening to the youth, who was walking with me at the time.

We had gone about 100 yards or so, when I looked down and saw another rock similar in shape but smaller, and also broken in half. I bent down and picked it up, not really looking at it right then, but thinking to myself that it would be so neat to have 2 mountain scenes on 2 similar rocks on my desk, never mind the desk of one of the parents. (Yup, even we Youth Leaders have some motives that are borderline). I was pretty intent on listening to the youth that was walking with me at the time, so I didn't give it much more thought right then. We had walked and talked for a while, when all of a sudden, I realized that the two rocks were actually one and the same. The second rock I had found was the other half of the first one. Incredible, what were the chances of that happening? Maybe one in a gigazillion, if that: pretty neat GOD.

Well, that was pretty neat, by itself, but things got even better. The first was that the weather held and we didn't need to paint the rocks, which was another blessing. You see, I was so afraid that I might have to show off my totally non existent art skills. GOD allowed me grace this time by not humbling me in front of the youth group and the leaders. My humbling time was to come later.

The next morning, Sunday, I asked one of the leaders what he had prepared for the Sunday message. His reply was, "Well, I thought we would sing this, this and then end off with, It Only Takes A Spark To Get A Fire Going." Great I said, but what are you going to talk on. "Talk on," he asked rather perplexed, "I'm not talking, all I'm doing is singing, you are doing the message." Oh no! He had misunderstood my direction to him and all he had prepared was some songs. Now what! So I grabbed my bible and headed off to be by myself to seek GOD and ask His guidance for a message that would bring this trip to a great close for the youth, leaders and me.

DECISIONS

I remember sitting at one of the picnic tables in the campsite reading my Bible and praying. Asking GOD what to say and I kept getting this message that I was to go and chop wood. "Chop Wood! Come on GOD, get real, I'm trying to prepare a message about how real you are, and how you can be real in these kids lives. Chop wood; ya right." The message came again, and it came again. Finally in shear desperation, I went to the cook shack and picked up my axe and chopped one piece of wood in half. "There, are you satisfied" I half yelled into the air. "NO keep chopping" came the reply. I went to grab another piece of wood and the message was, "Finish the one you started on." So I kept chopping until all I had was a pile of kindling. Then all of a sudden, God reveled a small part of the message to me. Thank you GOD! I picked up the pile of kindling and turned to leave the cook shack, when I spotted the 2 pieces of rock I had found the day before. I reached up and put them in my pocket for a reason yet unknown to me, and headed for the main fire pit where the youth had already gathered for the Sunday noon service. I still did not know the full message that God would give me. But I trusted fully that He would provide the message as I needed it.

Now we need to back up just a bit here. You see, the night before we had a big fire in the fire pit;

sang songs, talked, shared, laughed and even cried. At midnight, we had put the fire out and moved all the logs to the outside edge of the pit. Like good boy scouts would do right. It is now 12 hours later and we are in the mountains, where it gets really cold at night, and I mean cold when we got up that morning we had ice on our tent ropes and frost on the grass. So believe me when I say the fire pit was stone cold. We started to sing songs, with the last song being, It Only Takes A Spark. Before we started to sing, I asked the youth to each pick up a piece of kindling, and I asked Brad, one of the youth, to place each piece that was handed to him in the fire pit. Brad was our Mr. Woodsman, Boy Scout and lifeguard all in one. After Brad had placed the kindling in the middle of the fire pit, we started to sing, It only takes a spark, and we just got into the second verse when the kindling burst into flames. There was no smoke to warn of an impending fire, but there it was. Have you got duck bumps yet? I did! I still do, I could hardly finish playing the song on my guitar let alone sing the song. I was bouncing up and down and praising GOD for all I was worth. (Of course all this jumping and praising God was purely internal. As I am sure you are aware that Youth Leaders must remain perfectly calm at all times and in all circumstances. Especially in times like this one that reflects the real power of GOD).

DECISIONS

Ya right, like as if, eh!

It was incredible, the fire pit was dead dog cold, there were no matches to be seen. Yet the fire started, and I mean started! Even the hair on my arm stood up and paid attention. This was something big. We finished singing the song and the youth were kind of in shock, my tongue was stuck to the roof of my mouth and we watched the fire slowly burn down as the kindling burnt up. None of us were really able to move or speak after this great demonstration of God's power. Then GOD gave me the message, and I spoke.

"The cold fire pit is just like our lives when we walk away from GOD and out of His will. We carefully pull all the hot coals out of the center of our lives and move them to the side so that we can get on with the so called more important things like, parties, friends, work, fast cars, faster women and bars. The fire in our hearts that was there because of JESUS living inside us is put out by us, as we look to other temporal and worldly things to please us, to meet our needs. But just as with the kindling in the fire pit that GOD just lit, when we add kindling to our lives, (the word of GOD, fellowship, prayer), the fire is relit. But look at the fire; . . . it's going out." I asked some of the youth to add some more kindling to the fire, and we watched as the fire grew. "Do you see how we need to feed our spiritual life, just as the fire needs fuel to keep going?" Everyone of the group nodded affirmation. I reached into my pocket and pulled out the 2 pieces of rock and held them together as though they were one. "Just as this rock used to be 1 rock, the relationship between God and man was one. Then sin came into the world and it split the relationship between God and man; just as this rock has been split in two. GOD was not happy with this, so after many years of trying to get His people, (us), to listen and see all that He had provided for them, He sent His son JESUS CHRIST to die on the cross for all of our sins. Jesus Christ became the glue to bring our relationship with God back into one." Jesus Christ is the rock we have learned to build our lives on. On solid rock I will stand.

Too Much! GOD had provided the material way before the message and it all fit. Get the message?

GOD was answering prayer in other parts of my life as well, ways that were blowing my mind: covering my wife in an emergency C section with **NO** anesthetic. Talk about my mind being blown, . . . you should have seen the Doctors and Nurses on that one. . . . Watching the Doctors cut my wife open;

DECISIONS

with no anesthetic is not my idea of fun. The baby, (our daughter), was in distress and they could not use a general anesthetic, because I have a genetic deficiency that doesn't allow my body to break down general anesthetics. This means that the baby could also be deficient in this area. No time to do a spinal, because the baby was in such distress. My wife asked the Doctor what she could expect to feel during the surgery. His reply was that she would scream in pain, get violently ill and pass out. So we prayed, and I believed GOD would answer. We prayed Philippians 4:13 "I can do all things in CHRIST who strengths me." Over and over again we prayed that verse. The Doctor, who was sitting a few feet away, came close so he could hear what was happening. So close that his head was resting on mine just above my wife's. After the operation, he came to me and said, "I've never seen anything like that before in my life. It was like there was someone there taking all her pain away. Every time you prayed, her face would go from ashen grey to pink. And then before you could begin to pray again, her face was ashen grey again, then pink. It was like there was someone there taking all her pain away." "There was," I said, "His name is JESUS CHRIST." To which he just walked away, muttering under his breath, "I've never seen anything like it before."

Praise GOD! So here I was seeing how GOD was working in the lives of those around me and feeling so great to be involved in some small way. And all the while not knowing that I was missing it all, by a distance of less than 18 inches: the distance from my brain to my heart.

During all these things that were happening, my wife became my tower of strength. Without realizing it, I began to look to her instead of to God for everything. I had called her my gift from God, because she had led me back to the Lord after a very long time on my own. So I had begun to look to her for my support, love and guidance. Only later would God show me how unfair this was to her and more importantly unfair to God. I still do call her my gift from God, only I have learned to look to God to provide my needs now, support, love and guidance in the form of wisdom.

Chapter Two

The Dentist

With all these great things going on, I went to the Dentist on August 22nd, 1994, for a routine root canal operation. But something went wrong; I had an allergic reaction to the anesthetic, and went into anaphylactic shock, followed by respiratory arrest. Which in essence, means I was not breathing. Without air you can not live, which means I died for those of you out there that need it spelt out. Now I am sure that some of you out there are saying, ya, well I can hold my breath for 2 minutes. Great, I am glad for you, but I was well past being able to hold my breath. I had been struggling for air for some time before I stopped breathing. Which means that I didn't have that great big last breath to hold onto. No 2 minute bell for me. Life for me at that moment ceased to exist. **I was DEAD!**

I have been assured that my death was a very short lived death. What a statement! Let me assure you that any time this happens; it is a traumatic event in ones life and the life of those around you. But, also let me tell you, to me that short lived death felt like it lasted a life time. I remember the Dentist and his assistants fighting to save me. The whole clinic became this finely tuned team. Putting an oxygen mask over my mouth and bagging me trying to get air into my screaming lungs, checking my pulse and respirations. The Dentist stuck a needle of adrenalin into my thigh. I Heard the Nurse, (the mother of two of the youth from the youth group I led), pleading, "breath, . . . breath Kim, . . . breath." Then watching the Dentist turn away and hide his head as I breathed, what I thought, was my last breath. I remember thinking this was such a dumb way to go. It looked just like a movie, fading to black as the commercial is coming on, but no commercial came on. Was this how it was to end?

DECISIONS

But wait a minute, if it is the end, how come I am thinking? It was all so confusing. Then this warm feeling: a feeling of love and acceptance like I have never felt before or since. My eyes opened and the room was so incredibly bright, like stars all around me. I felt this flurry of activity around me, which I now attribute to being my guardian Angels holding me up. I started to look around me, but everything seemed out of place. I didn't realize at first that I could look down, but when I did, I was shocked. I could see the whole room below me, everyone, even me, or at least my body. There I was lying on the chair, but I wasn't there. I was up above looking down at me. What was happening to me? I looked so silly, just lying there. Hey, there is the Dentist with his back to me, the two (2) Dental Nurses looking down with tears in their eyes. The front receptionist, who was standing behind me, was holding my wife, trying to comfort her, and my wife looking on in total disbelief. She looked so incredibly beautiful, so scared, and so all alone . . . ANGER! It boiled up inside of me. Even with all this love that surrounded me, I remember feeling so angry! **Why now God! ! !** GOD; . . . don't let me die like this, . . . I'll do better, . . . my wife and daughter, . . . **I** need them.   **I** need to feel their love, and give them mine. Let **me** go back! . . . **PLEASE! ! !** . . . Let **me** go back!

Just as I said that; the Dentist in what appeared to be a moment of anger or shear desperation turned and delivered a second injection of adrenalin into my right thigh. And at that same moment, I started to breath again. I remember holding up my right hand with my thumb in the air signaling the Dentist I was okay. But more importantly, signaling to myself that I was back. I could feel the tension in the room, the shock, the relief and most of all I felt my total disbelief about what had just happened. Even to the point of denial by all, especially me. I was afraid to face what had happened. I was the Ostrich, bury your head in the sand and it will go away. Don't think about it or much worse talk about it. Deny its reality and it won't exist. What a joke eh! From that moment on that brief experience of death was to haunt me for nearly 12 years, and totally change the rest of my life.

The paramedics arrived on scene at this time and took over. Placing me on oxygen and doing an EKG strip, moving me from the Dentist chair and placing me on the stretcher and then the lights and sirens to the Rockyview Hospital. Where they did more tests, placing ice packs on my right thigh where the Dentist had given the injections that saved my life, and having me breathe oxygen with ice to ease the

DECISIONS

pain in my chest. They told me that all was well and to go home and rest.

I felt anything but well. I was scared silly, but too proud to admit it and so I tried the old male macho thing of "Who ME Scared!" Ya I was scared. My life all of a sudden became way too delicate. Where I used to be fearless, (some people actually told me I had a death wish because of my total lack of regard for my safety). Now it was like I was in this fragile glass jar with only this very thin transparent layer of glass between me and death. All too real, and all too scary. Life became precious at that moment.

When, I got home from the Hospital the phone was ringing. It was the Hospital calling to say they had made a mistake and they wanted me back at the Hospital ASAP. No mention as to what was wrong or why, just that they had made a mistake and wanted me back. Now we are talking scared!

I remember trying so hard to maintain control. Even to the point of insisting on driving myself back to the Hospital. No sense in getting my wife uptight over a phone call right? Just after arriving back at the Hospital I experienced the first of 4 heart attacks. Which in case any of you are in any doubt of, I did survive them all, no down time if ya catch my drift. I have been told that my heart attacks were considered medically induced and hence not as life threatening as a heart attack that occurs because of a blockage in the flow of blood to the heart. However any heart attack is still considered serious, especially when you are the one that is having it.

So here I am in the Hospital trying to maintain control, and looking for someone from the Church to come and save me. And no one came. Director of Youth Ministry for 3 plus years you say. Where was everyone? Did **I** really matter? Wasn't **I** as important as **I** thought **I** was, ... Did GOD even really care? So my focus came right off of GOD and onto what **I**, **Kim Proudlock** could or couldn't do! Well, for just over a year, **I** found out that all **I** could do was mess things up big time. And mess things up might be just a little bit of an under statement. **I** really messed things up. The secular world has a term for this, called FUBAR. I like the idea, but not the exact term. So I have decided to call it MUBAR, (messed up beyond all recognition). That was definitely me, **MUBAR!**

Chapter Three

Alone and Lost

I experienced heart damage from all this and I also suffered from a spiraling depression. The longer everything went on, the worse things got. To the point where things happened like not knowing who the woman I was sleeping with was, (my wife), not knowing the difference between things like eggs and oranges. I couldn't do math, 2 + 3, not a clue. A telecommunications specialist by trade and I had no idea about math, bizarre. I would go for a drive and not know how I ended up where I did. Let alone how I got there. Or where I was coming from, to get to where I got, (and I thought I was mixed up then. After reading that, you probably have doubts about me even now)!

I remember driving down the road one day and seeing a sign that said right lane closed ahead and wondering which way was right, and being totally panicked, to a point where I had to stop the car and sit and wait for someone to tell me where to go. . . . And I was so glad when they didn't tell me how to get there to! . . . Then while showering, I felt this weird fuzzy thing on my face and I started screaming in absolute terror, not realizing that during my recovery that I had grown a beard. Ya, I'd looked at myself in the mirror, but never really saw who was looking back at me. . . . Mubar, just total mubar, I was messed up beyond all recognition. And still the question, . . . why GOD? Why if you let me come back did I come back like this? Who is this person in the mirror that I do not recognize? Who is this GOD that I have called out to all this time? Who used to answer me? Where is He? Why

DECISIONS

isn't He here with me when I need Him the most? WHY? These questions and many more plagued my mind and filled my every thought. Many times I would actually scream out to GOD in anger and frustration begging for answers to all my questions. Was anyone home up there? It sure didn't seem like it!

It took me almost 4 months to the day to tell anyone about my experience on the Dentist chair. I was pretty sure if I told anyone, they would commit me and I would be in the rubber room forever. The person I chose to tell was my wife. After all, if you can't trust your wife who can you trust, right? In most cases I pray that is true, however, for me it appears now to have been the start of my undoing. My wife was in the same belief pattern that I had been in. I had felt that anyone that had a so called out of body experience had been taking some very heavy drugs, for way too long and was maybe more than just a little crazy. So when my wife reacted so adamantly with, "Don't tell anyone, especially my folks!" Panic struck, I am crazy. I have gone over the edge and I am crazy. From that day on, I began to doubt everything that I saw and everything that I heard. Little did I know, that by doing that, (closing myself off), I unintentionally opened myself up to even more problems. Hiding who you are and what you are feeling is not the answer. GOD gave each of us feelings, but more importantly, he gave us the ability to choose how we respond to those feelings. Hiding those feelings was and still is a bad choice.

I had been hearing voices for sometime now since my accident at the Dentist. Many nights, I lay awake all night listening to the voices talking in the living room of our house. I could not hear what they were saying, it was like a distant buzz, and every time I tried to get out of bed to see what was going on, the voices would stop. I even felt like there was a presence everywhere I went on the acreage that we were renting. But most notably I could feel it in the house and the path between the house and the barn. Many times it was like I would run into things between the house and the barn and I would fall down. Or all of a sudden, I would loose my balance for no apparent reason. I kept saying that the bruises I was getting were from the drugs I was taking. The drugs were causing me to loose my balance. Yet all the while knowing that it was something else; but too afraid to admit it or deal with it. Hide Kim, hide!

One evening, my wife, daughter and I were at home and this is what happened.

DECISIONS

I was walking from the living room into the kitchen area. I got to the doorway and I could see my daughter in her highchair to my right. My wife was just out of my sight at that time, somewhere towards the left of the door. When I entered the kitchen, our big double fridge was on my left side and just as I got to the front of the fridge, a force hit me so hard it sent me back into the living room and I landed flat on my backside. My wife who had been down on the floor at the pantry just out of my view had looked up just as I entered into the kitchen and saw what happened and began to scream. I picked myself up and ran into the kitchen to see what was going on and I could not calm her down. It wasn't until much later after we had put our daughter to bed that I asked her what the matter was. "Didn't you see it" she asked? "See what" I replied, because I had seen nothing. So she proceeded to tell me that when I came into the kitchen, she looked up just before I was sent flying and that a black shadow went right in front of me. "Didn't you see it?" It must have been what pushed me, no wonder she was scared. Listening to her and what she saw sure had me scared. I remember feeling like I was truly losing it and thinking that no one really cared or would even really miss me. The thought process of suicide started here. Here where core values had been stretched to the limit, where even my wife was wondering about this man she was married to. What was going to happen next?

I was scared stiff. Here is a couple that already had a lot on their minds trying to deal with all the things that I was going through and then this happens. What was going on? I didn't know, but I did know that it was beyond anything that we could deal with, so I called the Pastor of the Church we were attending at the time and asked for help. He arranged a meeting with 2 very senior Pastors, himself, my wife and I for the very next day. They came over and I described everything that had been happening since my trip to the Dentist. But that I had been afraid to tell anyone, because they would feel I was crazy. (Which by the way where are you right now? Some of you I am sure are calling 9-1-1 for me right now. Others are praying. What ever you are doing, I thank you for caring)?

I told them how I was especially afraid that my wife would feel that I was crazy, considering her reaction with the out of body experience, she must have been absolutely scared silly with all this going on now. I even doubted how the Pastor's would handle all this. The Pastor's all agreed that it was definitely something that required prayer and we

DECISIONS

started out with me praying and ensuring that I was right with GOD, followed by some corporate prayer by all of us. When they were ready to leave, my doubting wife, who I credit with great wisdom said. "Isn't someone going to pray for the house?" Such great wisdom my wife showed with that question. The Pastor's agreed and we started in the bedroom, preceded through the house into the kitchen. Where my wife and I were standing against the kitchen cupboards facing the fridge and the 3 Pastors were to our left. One of the Pastor's was praying and all of a sudden GOD laid it on his heart to pray for the fridge. He said, "Satan, if you are residing in the fridge, I command you by the power of the blood of JESUS CHRIST to flee this house now!"

Once again a force hit me so hard, I was physically pushed against the cupboards with my back pushed so far back that my head and shoulders were touching the upper cabinets. It was like I was being forced out of the house right through the wall. My wife reached out and grabbed me, just as GOD said to me, "You will bow down and give thanks for what has just happened." In my fear and my pride, I said, "No GOD, I can't do that in front of these men of God." "You will bow down and give thanks for what has just happened here," and again I said no. This time GOD took all the strength from my legs and I folded on the floor with my wife hanging onto me. And I gave thanks to the LORD our GOD for who he was and what he had done.

The 2 senior Pastors' came over and laid hands on me and prophesied over me saying, "Your name has been forever rewritten in the Lamb's book of life. Your name is no longer Kim Proudlock, but Kim Humblelock, for you have been humbled in the eyes of the LORD."

What an incredible prophecy. If only I had been able to take it to heart and fully understood that by being humbled, I needed to call out to GOD for help and not look to the Church, Pastors, friends, or my wife to save me. The job of saving me had already been filled by Jesus Christ. But I didn't understand that yet. I needed to be humbled once more before it would start to come together for me.

Here I was in the middle of this very real spiritual battle, something I had never seen before or believed was possible and it really scared me. This was something I was sure that never existed and yet it sure was real, I had the bruises to prove it, both on my body and my mind. Looking back on this,

DECISIONS

I truly feel that this is where my wife and I parted: neither one of us knew how to handle what was happening and we were once again left on our own to struggle through it. With both of us pulling away from the other because of what we could not understand. My poor wife I am sure must have felt that I was demon oppressed, and somewhat crazy to boot. And I, well I just felt that MUBAR fit me more and more each and every day. This spiritual warfare stuff is pretty heavy stuff, even to someone who is balanced in their day to day life. Let alone me in the condition that I was in.

Ephesians 6:10 - 12 (NIV)

"Finally, be strong in the Lord and in his mighty power. Put on the full armor of God so that you can take your stand against the devil's schemes. For our struggle is not against flesh and blood, but against the rulers, against the authorities, against the powers of this dark world and against the spiritual forces of evil in the heavenly realms."

Do you believe in the Bible as the inspired word of GOD? Then believe in spiritual warfare my friends. If I had known then what I know now thanks to

God, I may have been able to pull myself out of where I was then headed for. But perhaps I needed to go even further to find true peace. But please believe that spiritual warfare is real and we need to read on in Ephesians 6:13 - 18, where God tells us to put on the full armor of God so we can do battle with the evil one.

Ephesians 6:13 -18 (NIV)

"Therefore put on the full armor of God, so that when the day of evil comes, you may be able to stand your ground, and after you have done everything, to stand. Stand firm then, with the belt of truth buckled around your waist, with the breastplate of righteousness in place, and with your feet fitted with the readiness that comes from the gospel of peace. In addition to all this, take up the shield of faith, with which you can extinguish all the flaming arrows of the evil one. Take up the helmet of salvation and the sword of the spirit, which is the word of God. And pray in the Spirit on all occasions with all kinds of prayers and requests. With this in mind, be alert and always keep on praying for all the saints."

DECISIONS

In the Life Application Bible, it has the following explanation of the above text. "In the Christian life we battle against rulers and authorities (the powerful evil forces of fallen angels headed by Satan, who is a vicious fighter, see I Peter 5:8). To withstand their attacks, we must depend on God's strength and use every piece of his armor. Paul is not only giving this counsel to the church, the body of Christ, but to all individuals within the church. The whole body needs to be armed. As you do battle against "the powers of this dark world," fight in the strength of the church, whose power comes from the Holy Spirit. These who are not "flesh and blood" are demons over whom Satan has control. They are not mere fantasies - they are very real. We face a powerful army whose goal is to defeat Christ's church. When we believe in Christ, these beings become our enemies, and they try every device to turn us away from him and back to sin. Although we are assured of victory, we must engage in the struggle until Christ returns, because Satan is constantly battling against all who are on the Lord's side. We need supernatural power to defeat Satan, and God has provided this by giving us his Holy Spirit within us and his armor surrounding us. If you feel discouraged, remember Jesus' words to Peter: "On this rock I will build my church, and the gates of Hades will not overcome it" (Matthew 16:18)."

So the battle is real my friends, it is one that we can only engage in once we have put on the full armor of God. So I encourage you, before you go any further in my story to put on the full armor of God and ask for his guidance and protection. Because I didn't, I almost lost my all. I did however lose my family, and many of my friends in the process. Something I wish I could change, but it will forever be a brush stroke on my life that will affect me daily.

So in my ever increasing need to maintain control, I succeeded in pushing my wife away from me. Something that to this day I wish I had not done. I verbally struck out in anger trying to invoke some sense of feeling, some kind of a response, looking for love and to find new meaning to my life. Yet in doing so I was pushing those who loved me away and not even knowing I was doing it or why. After almost a full year of being like this, and being on tons of medications, (up to 23 at once). I came close to having both my kidneys and liver quit on me. The Doctors made a monumental decision at that time to remove me off all drugs and to start me on just one drug at a time. However in hind sight, I feel that they should probably have given me a

DECISIONS

week or so with no drugs before they began their new line of attack, in an effort to allow my body to clean out all the poison that was in me from being over drugged in the first place.

They seemed to feel that what at this time was being classified as depression was my most important area to be worked on. However, the first drug they tried me on, I said, "Man you just gotta get me off this stuff, because it makes me really aggressive," boom off the drug I was and right on to the next one. And right away I said, "Man you gotta get me off this stuff, because it makes me sleep 24 hours a day." Boom off that drug. Then right on to the next drug and I said "Boys get me off this thing because all I can do is think of suicide". Well you guessed it, they said no way, and you have to stay on this one for at least 6 weeks. . . . **WHAT!**

For almost 6 weeks I begged them to take me off the stuff. I actually went off it myself for a while but when they found out about it they doubled my dosage and then, I was total **M U B A R ! ! !**

J. K. Proudlock

Chapter Four

Count Down to Suicide

I remember talking to my wife very early in August 1995, and saying. "I've got it all worked out, I'm going to commit suicide on August 18th." Very quietly without even looking at me she said, "Why the 18th." "Well", I said, "I am doing music ministry at the Church, (this was a new Church we were attending, in Langdon, just outside of Calgary), for the next 2 weeks, and then my Moms birthday is on the 17th and after that no one has any   for me." My wife just turned away and said nothing. I can't imagine the pain she must have felt with my statement. In effect, I was telling her that she didn't love me. Here she was, hurting just as much if not more than I was, through this whole thing, and I go and say something so hurtful.

 I remember feeling like a total failure at that point. Life had nothing to offer and all I wanted to do was end my life. Remove myself from her life so that she didn't have to go through with something drastic like a divorce. You see I know what kind of scars a divorce leaves on a person, and I didn't want my wife to have those scars on her. Even though at that time I was so hurt by her reaction, or more to the point, what I perceived as a lack of reaction to my statement of my impending suicide, I loved my wife; more than my own life. The words JESUS spoke came to mind, "**Greater love has no one than this, that he lay down his life for his friends**" John 15:13 (NIV). I truly thought that the only way I could show my love to her was by dying and removing this parasite, . . . me, from her life.

Suicide, . . . such a seductive word, it can peak

DECISIONS

ones interest, get their belly boiling, heart
pounding, stressed to the max. Every emotion given
to man is active and each and every one of us will
react in a different way, it's like the word cancer
was 20 years ago. Cancer still scares us, but most
of us can talk about it now. But Suicide, . . . well,
that one simply freaks just about all of us. I was in
her deadly grasp. Suicide, I was being lulled into a
feeling of security. "End your life, it is the only way
to ease the pain, free yourself and all those around
you." It was like a drug gripping my mind and taking
control of all my thoughts, how could I escape it?

A lot of things happened over the next couple of
days and none of them very good. My wife was
having just as much trouble dealing with where I
was and what I had said I was going to do as I was.
And just as I dealt with my pain in one fashion, she
began to deal with her pain in another. She began to
spend money. Kind of like when the going gets tough
the tough go shopping. Even now I am not able to
understand her reaction, but I can not fault her for
it, her pain was just as real as mine. I dealt with my
pain one way and she dealt with hers in another.
Neither of us was right in how we handled it. And
just as I must live every day with the consequences
of my actions, she is still living with hers.
Finally on August the 7th, 1995 I decided that was

it. NO MORE! I was going to do myself in on that day. Why delay what was meant to happen. My wife had told me some things from her past the night before, in what I believe was an effort to cleanse herself of them. I think she felt that I was truly going to kill myself and that by telling me these things she would have told someone with skin on and hence she would not be bound by them any longer. I did not have the power then, and I still, (thank GOD), do not have the power now to cleanse her of her sins. Only GOD can do that. Only GOD can forgive! Through the blood of His son JESUS CHRIST we come washed and clean into the presence of GOD. No human can take that upon themselves; no human can expect another human to be able to do what only GOD can do!

At the time that she told me about these things, I could not deal with them. I was repulsed, disgusted, and hurt, but in looking back, they were no worse than anything that I have done in my life time. But I could not stand to see my wife in so much pain, and I felt it was my entire fault. So after my wife left for work, I started to make some phone calls. I called Ken, my best friend, he had been my best man at our wedding and told him today was it. I was going to blow up the house, stick a hose from the exhaust of my truck into the cab, hang myself, slit

DECISIONS

my throat, whatever it took, I couldn't handle any more of my life being torn away from me. Ken knowing where I was at called my wife at work. At that time, she was the last person that I wanted to talk to. I was feeling very hurt by what I felt was a lack of care and concern on her part, and the things she had just told me were still tearing me apart inside. I felt she had already given up on me: I was just a useless, sick old man, a burden that no one needed, especially my wife. So to get rid of her, I pushed all the buttons that I knew would hurt. I was a real jerk. My wife was really concerned, because I was at home with our 1 year old daughter, and in my condition, I might have done something that might have brought harm to her. So her reaction to call for help from the hospital was a good one. I offer prayers of thanks to God often on her part because of that phone call.

When the PAS Clinic of the Foothills Hospital called me and talked to me, we came to a deal. If I would come in, they would admit me and change my drugs, and ensure that I was helped before they released me; TOO good to be true man. This is what I had been begging for. So off I went to the Foothills Hospital. I was really bent out of shape when I got in there. I did some real dumb things, like phoning AGT and asking them to disconnect my home phone line, fighting with my sister on the phone. All the while calling out for love and if I saw any, turning and running from it as fast as I could. Just way too confused and scared. Wanting so badly to fit in and feeling like I was never going to fit in again.

I remember the 8th day that I was in the Hospital, I came running out of my room screaming with joy, "I can add, I can add, I know what 2 plus 3 is. I can add!" They had lived up to their promise that they would change my medications when I was admitted, and it worked. For the first time I felt like there was hope. Maybe, just maybe, I could be the person that I used to be: even more loving, tender and kinder. Maybe even a better husband and father. That would be so cool. Yet in all my happiness, not once did I acknowledge God, or thank Him for His healing hand in all this.

The nurses, had been giving me lots of time to talk and helping me understand some of the things that were going on in my life, and I was feeling much better. Not on solid ground, but much better. I was still leaning on man and mans ability to heal me; GOD was only allowed into a very small part of the equation, and only if I let Him. The Psychiatrist told me that I needed to call my wife and ask her to meet with me. And to have her make a list of all the concerns that she had and that I would make a list

DECISIONS

of my concerns, so that we could talk about them. He also told me that he was not going to discharge me until both my wife and I had counseling together, so we could both learn to deal with what was going on.

GREAT, that is just what I had been trying to get all along. So I called and arranged to meet with my wife the next day and to have someone look after our daughter while we talked. I remember being so excited and feeling like a kid, wanting so badly for everything to go well. And it did for the first bit then tension arose, when I asked my wife some very pointed questions about her past and where we stood now. Talking ceased and our wonderful meeting was over. I could really feel tension from my wife, she was scared about what I might do and really unsure about where to go from where we were at. Unsure about if she could handle who I was, at that time. I am sure that some of the questions that I asked her, especially the ones that she avoided answering put some guilt on her; guilt that she did not hide very well and guilt that put my already sick mind into overdrive as I attempted to deal with the reality of my wife's unfaithfulness.

So I went back to my hospital room and the joy I had the day before of being able to do math was becoming very distant, and the thought of loosing my wife was becoming way too real. The next morning, after going off ward for 15 minutes, I returned to have the nurses tell me that I had 45 minutes to pack up and leave. I had been discharged. WHAT!!! I couldn't believe it, so I called the Dr. and he replied saying, "I went home last night and slept on it and I feel you are okay to go home." Don't do this to me I begged, I'm not ready. Please! Not a chance, I had to be out of there in 45 minutes. I still don't understand why that decision was made. To be perfectly honest, anything the medical profession tells me now is questionable in my mind. But all the medical questions aside, let's get back to my story.

I called my wife and told her that I had been discharged and that I would catch a bus to her work to pick up my truck. I could feel her apprehension in my calling her and she became very adamant that I wait until she came and picked me up at the Hospital. So I finally agreed. When she came to pick me up, I was feeling a mixture of joy and fear. Joy at being out of the Hospital, and FEAR because I knew I wasn't ready to be out and especially being picked up by my wife. I had a feeling something was in the air. Well, it didn't take much time after she picked me up to find out that

DECISIONS

there was definitely something up. She wanted to go for coffee and talk. **T A L K,** my heart sank into the pit of hell. Right then and there, I knew that she was leaving me. The last thing I wanted to do was to Talk. I needed to be held. Heck I needed to be back in the Hospital, back where there was security, someone to talk to, and someone who would listen to me. So needless to say, we didn't talk, at least not in a productive sort of way. I left her at her office, parked in her car, crying and I headed home in my truck, neither one of us very happy; both of us probably just wanting to have things back to normal, whatever that may have been.

When I got home, I found the house all packed up. My wife was leaving me, just as I had suspected. I was devastated, confused and very angry. I called her at work and asked her what was up; her reply was that she couldn't live with me any more. Great, just what I didn't need. It was however what she needed, and at the time I could not see that! All I could see was poor little old me, the hole that I was falling into was getting so much deeper, and there appeared to be no way out, and no bottom. What to do now? I could feel the desperation closing me in, I got so scared that I could hardly breathe!

One of the great things, (cough cough), that they had taught me in the Hospital was that if I got angry, I should throw things. Unbreakable things, but throw them none the less. Trust me, this may work for the odd, and I mean very odd person, but it did not work for me. I got angrier and angrier. The more I threw things on the floor the worse my mood was, until I looked at the mess I had created and became so angry, I knew that if I didn't leave right then and there I was going to do something that I would regret for the rest of my life.

So I loaded up the truck and moved on down the highway. Highway #1 that is, east bound, looking for that magical crude that would improve my mood. Sorry about that, I kind of got off on a Beverly Hill Billy kind of thing for a minute. But off down Highway #1 I headed. I picked up 2 hitch hikers who were heading to Saskatchewan and drove them all the way there. When I got there, I stopped for just a minute and reflected over what had just happened. I knew I was running away from my problems and that was not the answer. So I decided to turn around and head back home, with a certain amount of low level flying involved, if you catch my drift. When I got back to the Alberta border, I called my wife and left a message on the answering machine, simply saying, I was sorry and that I was

DECISIONS

on my way home. And when I got there, all I wanted
to do was listen to what she had to say. I needed to
understand what was going on. I needed to know
how this was affecting her, what I could do to help.
Could I do anything? I just needed to know!

Well, with the pedal to the metal, I managed to get
home right around 8:00 p.m.. I pulled up to the
corner at Langdon just as my wife, sitting in her
bosses van and another van driven by a coworkers
husband, (a City of Calgary Police Officer), arrived
at the same corner. All previous thoughts of
listening to my beautiful wife went out the window.
You see one of the questions that I had for my wife
back at the Hospital was, "Are you having an affair
with your boss?" There she was, sitting in his van,
no question in my mind any more. She had already
made up her mind to leave me and was going to be
with HIM! The old mind was in overdrive, processing
on a very dysfunctional CPU, and processing nothing
but very bad thoughts. 99% of them were probably
not even close to the truth, but at that time, the
truth didn't matter. All that mattered was my pain,
and how her leaving me was affecting me.

When we got to the house, I was confused about
what to do. I had locked my keys in the house, so
that my wife would not be afraid of me returning

and causing a scene. So how do I get in the house and keep these people out. I didn't want my wife to leave me. She was my gift from God, how could she leave me. How could God allow this to happen? Was there really a God? If there was, He really can't be all that concerned about me, my wife, and my family. All I wanted out of life was to have a family that loved me, a family that would be there with me to the end. But I guess this was the end. My wife is leaving me. I had failed!

So out comes the mean man, the ugly Kim Proudlock. The vengeful person lets point fingers, create pain to eliminate pain, if I was going to fail, so were those around me. I am so ashamed of that person, but there he was, me, yelling at the top of my lungs, telling all who were in hearing distance of all the confidences my wife had shared with me only weeks before. I was hurting so bad, and I wanted the world to hurt with me. I wanted my wife to hurt with me to. After all, she was the one that was leaving me. Lash out, take no prisoners.

I was so mean. I tried several times to talk to my wife, but the off duty Police man friend kept getting in my way. I wanted to pop him so bad. Here was a man that was trained to keep the peace and all he was doing was promoting a fight. It was as if

DECISIONS

he wanted to some how be a hero in all this. The
first time he put his hands on me, the rage inside of
me was so strong, it was all I could do not to drop
him where he stood. Then there was the boss man,
my wife's new source of strength, sitting in the
doorway to his van, calling the RCMP, to break up
this tense situation. What a wimp I thought, my
wife has left me for this wimp. Sure he has great
hair; he is younger, slim trim and all that. But he is
as gutless as they come. In all the time that I had
known him, he couldn't make a decision if his life
depended on it, a real fence sitter. Why don't I
just pop them all I thought? All but my wife that is.

Time to leave, things were just way too out of
control. Into the truck and gravel flying all over the
place, out the driveway. And then the truck stalls,
and everyone is looking at me. The thought of being
caught in an embarrassing situation like having a
vehicle break down, with witnesses has always been
a fear of mine. Here I was, me, the totally messed
up beyond all recognition person caught in just that
situation, sitting in my stalled truck with everyone
looking at me. So, I'll fix them. I'll scare the
stuffing out of them by racing into the driveway
and watch them all scatter. But they didn't scatter.
They just stood there. Why? I don't know, but I
almost hit all three of them. I was sick to my

stomach, I almost hit my wife. It would have been too bad about the other two, but my wife. Definitely time to leave. So off I drove, beating myself up even more because of my attitude and lack of control. I had become my worst nightmare, a man full of anger and bitterness. No wonder my wife was leaving me. No one could blame her now. She had the witnesses she needed to verify her need to leave me. Her story was safe now. No one would believe the things I had thrown back into her face about her past. My anger and actions had proven I was just crazy, right?

I really don't remember where I drove for the next couple of hours, I just drove. When I got back home about 10:30, the house was dark, no vans in the driveway, so I pulled in. I don't know if I am glad that my wife left the door to the house unlocked or not. You see, I had still left the keys to the house on the desk where I had placed them earlier that day. But it was unlocked, so I went in. I turned on the light switch and nothing happened. I tried another and still no lights. I couldn't understand what was happening. I found a flashlight and headed for the breaker panel, but I could see nothing wrong. Why weren't the lights working? I couldn't figure that one out. Here I am a Telecommunications Electrician and I can't get the

DECISIONS

lights to work. Mubar man, just plain mubar.

I decided that I needed some food, since I hadn't eaten since breakfast at the Hospital that morning and it was pretty late, I was plenty hungry. So I tried to turn on the gas stove, and it wouldn't work either. Frustration, anger, confusion, what is happening; nothing is working. The BBQ, I'll cook on the BBQ. I tried lighting the BBQ. Twice it lit and blew out. Great, just great, my wife has left me, the lights won't work, the gas stove won't light and now the BBQ won't light either. I am mubar, just totally mubar, as I continued beating myself up for things that were out of my control.

Now, thinking back and possibly thinking slightly more normal, I know that the smart thing would have been to get some take out food and gone home and cried in my pizza, K Fry, DQ or what ever I managed to get myself into. But on that night, I was not normal or anywhere near normal. I was mubar, just plain mubar. So off comes the propane tank, into the cab of my truck, (why inside, I still do not know), and off to Calgary to get it filled up.

 By the time I got into Calgary, all the places that I knew that sold propane were closed. Panic, frustration, feelings of total inadequacy, you name it, I was there. BUT, I had the presence of mind to call the Hospital and ask for help. "**HELP**! You have got to be kidding. Man you don't need help, grow up, get a life, go home and get some sleep. This is all situational; it will all be gone in the morning." This was the answer I got from the Hospital.

I felt so worthless, even the Hospital didn't care about my needs, my feelings, and my life. Where was this great medical system that Alberta/Canada was supposed to have. I didn't even rate a number on a scale of 1 out of Zillion. So off I drove, still looking for the one propane store that might be open. Thinking back, I'm sure that I probably passed 20 or 30 stations that sold propane and were open, but my mind was racing and not really on the supposed task at hand, finding propane. My thoughts were all over the gamut of what is going to happen to me now. What will my family think, what about the Church? My wife's family, friends, work, but most of all my wife. Thoughts of my wife consumed me. I wanted so much just to be with her, to feel the warmth of her against me, to see her smile and watch her sleep. I wanted to see her and my daughter playing, laughing, the good old times. But there would never be those good old times again would there? Not now. Now that she had

DECISIONS

found another. I felt so useless, so all alone.

About 2:30 a.m. on August 18th, I found myself outside the Foothills Hospital. I drove in and parked in the Emergency parking area and put money into the meter. I remember thinking, "How stupid to have meter parking in the Emergency area. Like who would remember to pay, if it was a real emergency. What are they going to do, tow your car away? How silly!" I went into the Hospital and walked right up to within 5 - 10 feet away from the admitting desk. It was like I hit a brick wall, I could go no further. There were 3 people behind the counter. All laughing, joking, looking up at me, but not one of them said anything to me. I felt like the biggest pile of manure this side of a pig farm. Why was I so bad that no one wanted to help me? I stood there looking at these 3 Hospital staff for over 5 minutes. I know it was this long based on how much time was left on the parking meter when I finally left. I turned and started to walk out, when I saw the pay phones. I called up to the Psychiatric Ward that I had just been discharged from and the Charge Nurse answered. "I'm down in Emergency and I need help, I can go no further. Please help me!" I pleaded. Her reply was "Oh Kim, if you really need help, get up and ask to see the Psychiatric Resident on duty. But really all you need is a good night's sleep. Why don't you just go home! It is all situational. Nothing to worry about." "NO! I need some help, sleep is just not going to do it, **I NEED HELP! ! !** I'm going to kill myself tonight, no this morning. I'm going to blow up my truck or do something." "How are you going to blow up your truck" she asked. "Well, I have an empty propane tank in my truck and I'll use it." "No Kim, you just need some sleep. Go Home." and the phone went dead. From that moment on, I knew that I was going to kill myself, unless someone really made an effort to help me. Someone who cared. But was there anyone out there who really cared, I questioned.

I walked out of the Hospital, and sat in my truck and watched the parking meter tick away; praying that someone who cared would show up and help me. The meter ran out, I started my truck and slowly drove out of the Hospital, still praying that someone would come out and stop me before it was too late. No one came, and off I drove.

When I left the Hospital, I saw a Shell service station down the street. It had one of those convenience stores attached and I thought they would have paper and such to write my notes of goodbye. I pulled into the lot and went into the

DECISIONS

store. The first thing I saw was a Bargain Finder News Paper. I knew how much joy my wife got out of reading the Bargain Finder, especially the horse section, so I picked one up. Next I bought a pad of paper, a package of envelopes and a package with 2 pens in it. Right next door to the Shell convenience store was a donut store, so I asked the fellow at the till if he would mind if I left my truck parked where it was while I went into the donut store. His reply was, "No problem, not much traffic at this time of night, so go right ahead. And thanks for asking." I went next door and bought a cup of coffee and sat down. I had no intention of drinking the coffee, but I knew that they wouldn't let me sit in there and write notes without buying something. So coffee it was.

The first note that I wrote was to my wife's boss. I figured if my wife and him were having an affair, I might have messed things up by what had happened earlier on that night. So in an effort to smooth things over, I wrote him a thank you note. Thanking him for being there for my wife when she needed someone, and to apologize for my attitude back at Langdon when he came to get my wife and daughter's things. I didn't want to have my wife lose her relationship with him due to me.

Next, I wrote a note to my wife. I had so much I wanted to say and it was blocked by anger. I wanted to tell her how much I loved her, how desperately I wanted things to be back to normal, but I had all this anger inside of me. So my attempts at trying to tell her about my love for her were buried in statements that pointed fingers at her. It was all her fault. She was leaving me. I rewrote my will and left everything to my wife, after all, she was the only one that I truly loved. I remember folding the note, with tears in my eyes, thinking I'll never see her smile again. That smile was all that I had lived for during the last 4 or 5 months. I took out the money I had in my wallet, my wedding ring and my watch that she had bought me just after we were married and stuffed it all in an envelope. After doing that and sealing the envelope, I thought better and took my watch back out. I hate so much not knowing what time it is, and having my watch on felt like a small comfort to me right then.

I left the restaurant and went back to the convenience store and left the unused note paper, envelopes and one unused pen with the attendant. He gave me a real quizzical look and I just said, "I'm sure you will have more need of these than I will," and I left. I still wonder if he thought I was totally crazy, or if maybe he knew what I had in mind; I

DECISIONS

guess I will never know the answer to that question along with a lot of other questions that I felt I needed answers to right then.

I got into my truck and drove to my wife's work place. Knowing that it would be closed and fully thinking that I would be able to deposit the envelopes between the double doors and stuff the Bargain Finder in the door handle somehow and then leave. When I got there, it was a little past 3:00 a.m. and I was just beginning to feel real tired. The envelope for my wife's boss went nice and easy between the double doors, and it fell to the floor on the inside. But when I tried to put the envelope for my wife between the doors, it wouldn't fit. What do I do now? I can't leave with just the note for my wife's boss sitting on the floor inside. I can't leave with the letter for my wife stuck in the door. There was cash, my wedding ring and most of all, the note to my wife and my revised will. I felt so stupid, all I could do was beat myself up, and the Mubar Man blew it again. I continued to beat myself up until I figured that the only way was to stuff the letter in the doors as best as possible. Put the Bargain Finder in the door handle and sit and wait for the arrival of my wife's co-workers. A feeling told me that my wife would not be in to work on this day. But I knew that the wife of the Policeman

arrived about 7:30 a.m. and I was pretty sure she
would be only too ready to get her fingers in the
pie. She seemed like the type.

So I pulled my truck back to the back of the lot
and waited, and waited. I wanted so much just to
leave, but I just couldn't with my letter stuck in
the door. So I waited.

 I pulled out my little new testament with Psalms
and Proverbs and opened it to Psalm 88.

Psalm 88 (NIV)

"O Lord, the God who saves me,
day and night I cry out before you.
May my prayer come before you;
turn your ear to my cry.
For my soul is full of trouble
and my life draws near the grave.
I am counted among those who go down to the pit;
I am like a man without strength.
I am set apart with the dead,
like the slain who lie in the grave,
whom you remember no more,
who are cut off from your care.

You have put me in the lowest pit,

DECISIONS

in the darkest depths,
Your wrath lies heavily upon me;
 you have overwhelmed me with all your waves.
You have taken from me my closest friends
and have made me repulsive to them.
I am confined and cannot escape;
my eyes are dim with grief.

I call to you, O Lord, every day;
I spread out my hands to you.
Do you show your wonders to the dead?
Do those who are dead rise up and praise you?
Is your love declared in the grave,
your faithfulness in Destruction?
Are your wonders known in the place of darkness,
or your righteous deeds in the land of oblivion?

But I cry to you for help, O Lord;
in the morning my prayer comes before you.
Why, O Lord, do you reject me
and hide your face from me?

From my youth I have been afflicted and close to
death;
I have suffered your terrors and am in despair.
Your wrath has swept over me;
your terrors have destroyed me.
All day long they surround me like a flood;

they have completely engulfed me.
You have taken my companions and loved one from
me;
the darkness is my closest friend."

This is such a lonely Psalm, and at first glance there
appears to be no answer from God. And that is what
I saw when I read it that night. No Answer. If only
I knew then the answer that God was giving me. If
I could have seen that he was with me through all
this pain and confusion. Things might have been
different. But this was where I was. God where are
you, where is my lover and friend that you have
taken from me; my wife. Answer me please!   Can
you feel my pain?   Do you see what I am about to
do?   If you are real show me!   I want to see
you!   Send someone to me.   Someone with skin
on, someone who cares. Or is there no one out there
who cares about me, just me? Am I so sick that no
one wants to have anything to do with me? This pain
I feel is real, yet no one understands. Why?   I
try to laugh it off, so that no one sees how much
pain I am in; so that I don't put them in a position
where they are outside of their comfort zone. But
I'm bleeding GOD! I'm bleeding all over, can't they
see? Or don't they want to. Is my pain too close to
them? Or am I too repulsive to them? Answer me
GOD, please, answer me.

DECISIONS

I remember sitting in my truck, I was freezing cold; too afraid to start it up, because I had left all my money in the envelope for my wife. I needed to have enough gas to drive away and do myself in. I saw the Calgary Police HAWKS helicopter flying search patterns directly south of where I was. Hope rose in me. The Hospital must have called the Police and they are looking for me. I flashed my headlights on and off for over 15 minutes, praying they would see and come and find me. But when they flew away, I began to realize that this was it. No one was going to come to help me, I was on my own.

My thoughts began to focus on how I was going to kill myself. I took a mental inventory of what I had and what it could be used for. I had an empty propane tank, big help that was going to be, no money to fill it. Well, there are all those level train crossings between here and Langdon. That was a possibility. Maybe, I'll try and just let myself freeze to death in my truck on some lonely stretch of back road. None of them sounded too appealing, but at least they sounded like an end. And an end is just what I wanted; an end to my pain and the pain that I was causing all those that I loved, especially my wife. The one person that I thought would never leave me. But she had left me. Because of the pain I brought into her life. But could I really blame her? After all, I was the MUBAR man.

I began to think about what I had of value in the truck. I had better leave it here, at my wife's work. Otherwise, the Greedy Police, (especially that good for nothing Policeman friend of my wife's), will take what they want and leave nothing to my wife. So I packed everything inside my jacket that I could find of value; my bible, wallet, spare change, empty pop bottles, maps, napkins etc.

Around 7:30 a.m., the policeman's wife arrived. Another co-worker arrived at the same time, and they both hurried into the shop. I felt like I must have the plague or something, the way they avoided me. I must be one real bad dude. I waited for a while still praying that they would come out and talk to me. Maybe they would be the person with skin on that would be able to talk me out of what I was going to do. But no one came out. What was it about me that was so repulsive? I still don't know.

At about 8:00 a.m., I started my truck and drove up to the front of the shop. I opened my door and threw my jacket, full of all my belongings, on the ground. All of my wife's co-workers were at the door looking at me, but no one said anything. So I

DECISIONS

said, "This is all I have left for my wife." and I drove off. When I got to the end of the Parking lot, I hit yet another brick wall. I could go no further. I looked back at my wife's co-workers huddled around the door of the shop; I looked all around and prayed, "God send someone to help me!" But there was no one around. I don't know why I did, but I reached over into the passenger seat and opened the valve of the propane tank sitting on the seat beside me. I could feel the rush of cold air. Still not knowing why I did it, I reached up to the dash of the truck and found matches. How they got there, I have no idea. I have never smoked in my life, (well not until that day anyway), and that really doesn't count does it? I sat there holding the matches and prayed again, "God send someone to help me!" There was still no one around.

BOOM ! ! !

I remember wondering what had happened, just as the explosion happened. Then I passed out. When I came to, the entire truck was on fire. I had no fear, none what so ever. No pain, and everything seemed like it was in slow motion. My seat belt was still on and the propane tank was still on the seat beside

me, shooting flames right at me and burning my
skin. I reached over and tried to unlock the driver's
door, and watched as the skin and meat from my
left hand stuck to the door and pealed off my hand.
I sat there looking at my hand and wondered why I
wasn't even worried that there still was no pain or
for that matter fear. I reached over to undo my
seat belt, and the propane tank fell to the floor,
shooting flames at my legs and feet. I got my seat
belt undone and reached for the power window
switch on the driver's door. It worked and I
climbed out of the window. Not realizing that the
force of the blast had blown the windshield
completely out of the truck. The back window and
passenger window were blown out as well. I had
absorbed most of the shock on the driver's side, so
that window was the only one still intact. The time I
spent trying to get that window down, was probably
under 5 seconds, but 5 seconds of fire can do a lot
of damage to a human body. The cab of the truck
was all disfigured from the force of the explosion.
The doors were bowed out and the roof of the cab
was all distorted. The flames were shooting 20 feet
into the air and licking the power and telephone
wires that were stretched between the poles that
my truck was parked under. That was some
explosion an empty propane tank caused!

DECISIONS

I stood there looking at my truck, not fully realizing what had happened. How did it blow up? I know I didn't light the matches. But I must have! How else could the truck have blown up? Boy if I tried to kill myself, I sure did a poor job. I am MUBAR, messed up way beyond all recognition. I looked back and saw all my wife's co-workers looking at me, but no one came to help. Time to get out of here and go for a walk to try and figure out what happened, not even really realizing that I was on fire and walking just created a friendly environment for the fire. More air.

I started to walk away and a man who had been driving a Handi-bus stopped and got out of his van and looked at me and asked, "Do you need a hand?" With parts of me still on fire this guy asks me, do I need a hand? Where do these people come from I thought. "Ya", I responded, "Ya got a gun" What a foolish question! This guy must have been as dumb as fresh road kill. Only something like that could be that dumb. So on I walked. Another fellow driving a black truck had parked it on the other side of the road and ran up to me and was hitting me with his baseball cap, trying to put out the fire, and asking me "What's your name, hey bud, what's your name."

As he walked along side of me, hitting me with his hat, trying to put out my smoldering clothes, which unfortunately gave more air to the fire that was still burning my body and clothes. At least he was making an effort though, more than my wife's co-workers who I knew and had worked with over the last year or more. I wish I knew who the man in the truck was, so I could thank him, but no where in the Police report, does it mention this man. Kind of makes you wonder what else was left out of the report. But, I would like to extend a huge **Thank You** who ever you are! I pray that God will bless you for your act of kindness in my time of need.

We continued walking to the bottom of the hill, where my legs finally gave out and I fell to the ground, where he proceeded to put the rest of my clothes out. He stayed there talking to me and trying to comfort me, while we waited for the ambulance. One of my wife's coworkers, (the wife of the Policeman), had followed me down the hill. She was afraid that somehow I was going to walk away from the scene of my attempted suicide and find a place to hide. When I first saw her, I was so angry. I felt she was laughing at me. The Mubar man. I am ashamed to say that I cursed her and

DECISIONS

called her all kinds of foul things. But, when I saw her tears, something inside me said, she isn't here to laugh at you man, she is concerned, scared. So, I started to tell her, that my wife wasn't the one that needed the help, it was me. I was the one that was hurting inside. My wife and my daughter weren't the ones in danger, it was me. I would never hurt them. Through her tears, she responded, "I know that Kim, I know." Yet all the while staying so far away from me as if not to catch what I had; whatever that was. I was so scared and all alone, even then. No one wanted to come near me except for this perfect stranger, who was being so kind to me. Why? What was so wrong with me that this was all happening? And the question went unanswered yet again, just as it had too many times in my life.

Right about then, the ambulance arrived. They were pretty good guys, but my attitude went south again real quick when I saw the wonderful loving Policeman, the husband of my wife's coworker. I was so angry with him still. But then it was as if God gave me this total sense of peace. I could feel how this must have shaken him up. My attempted suicide so close to his wife's place of work. He must be worried about his wife's safety, and my anger totally left me. Praise God; that was such a relief!

The ambulance attendants were afraid to move me, due to the extent of my burns. I told them to just stand by and watch as I moved myself onto the stretcher. They were so afraid of hurting me. Funny eh! Here I had just tried to take my life and these 2 caring ambulance attendants were afraid of hurting me. Life does have its idiosyncrasies'.

When they got me into the ambulance, they began the fight to stabilize me before transporting me to the Hospital. My veins had collapsed due to the massive loss of body fluids from the fire and they really had a go of it trying to get the I/V started. All the while they were doing this, I was trying to comfort them and assure them that they weren't hurting me. The guy that felt he was not needed was giving comfort in his own pain, how absurd. They tried getting an I/V started using all the normal places neck and arms, however my veins were not very good and they couldn't find one. So they decided to try my feet. Little did they know that the soles of my running shoes had melted to the bottom of my feet when I had knocked the propane bottle over in my attempt to unfasten my seatbelt. So when they took my runner off to try and get the I/V line running, the bottom of my foot stayed in my runner. I must have been in real shock, because all I could think of was, boy this brings a

DECISIONS

new meaning to running your feet off. Sick I know, especially in my circumstances. When I voiced this thought to the Ambulance attendants, in an attempt to help them deal with what was happening to me, I'm sure from how they looked at me that they felt I had left my rocker back in the truck. Yes, I was the MUBAR man.

Right about this time, the side door to the ambulance opened up and there was my most un-favorite policeman again. Anger stirred up inside of me again and almost as soon as it was there, God took it all away again. Why was God doing this? I really wanted to strike out at him. Make him feel the pain that I was feeling. Not the physical pain, but the over whelming mental anguish I was feeling. I had lost all of who I was; my wife, my daughter. He should feel this pain that I am feeling. Why should he get away scot free? But God gave me peace on this and I just looked at him, almost with pity. If he could only see what he had done, or better yet, what he could have done to prevent this. I pray somehow that he will learn from my mistakes, and the mistakes he made in dealing with me. So that he can deal with the next person in a more compassionate manner.

My policeman friend did not say much. He simply

asked if the ambulance attendants were ready to move me to the Hospital. To which they responded, "Soon", and he left. The ambulance ride was kind of hairy and I kept asking the guys to slow down and not risk getting hurt, or hurting anyone else. That didn't work, so I finally asked them to slow down so that I wasn't getting hurt. Because of my burns, I couldn't stabilize myself very well and every corner was an experience that I would rather forget. My arms were banging the sides of the stretcher and pieces of skin were being left all over. So when I put it to them that way, they slowed down and I started to go with the flow. The pain was getting so intense by this time that I was afraid that I was going to pass out. So I had to try and maintain a constant focus as to where I was and what was happening in order to stay awake. I had to stay awake. Memories of the Dentist flooded into my brain and I was sure if I closed my eyes I would die. And for some unknown reason, even with all the pain I was in right then, and the desire that I had only moments before, I did not want to die right then.

When we got to the Hospital, I remember the Nurses and Doctors being so kind to me. The Nurses were trying so hard to remove my medical alert Id bracelet from my right wrist and they

DECISIONS

were so scared of hurting me. I finally asked for a pair of tweezers and took it off myself. They couldn't believe that I was being so cooperative. One Nurse looked at me and choked off a gag reaction and said "My God, your fingers look like burnt BBQ'd wieners. I'll never be able to eat wieners again!" I guess I was quite a site, and not for sore eyes either.

The Doctors were mulling around and were really concerned about the fact that I had no hair in my nose. I'm thinking to myself, "Man these guys are really weird." Not until much later did I find out that if the nasal hair is burnt, there is a really good chance that the lungs have been damaged by the super heated air from the fire; which was the case with me. My nasal hair was totally non existent and my lungs were so badly damaged that they didn't think I was going to make it. How sick, here I survived a horrific explosion and fire to die from toasted lungs. I don't understand this God? Why?

About this time, the police came to interview me. I think I shocked them by being so candid about what had happened. They were concerned about the jacket that I had thrown out of the cab of my truck. They were sure that it had a bomb in it. "What are you guys nuts! If I had a bomb, I'd have used it on myself. Not left it lying on the ground 200 feet behind the truck." They were so convinced of this that they had their little robot out to pick up my jacket and toss it into the bomb trailer. What a bunch of goofs! But I guess they were only trying to be safe, or was it an opportunity to get some press on their little robot. Only the person in charge and GOD know the answer to that one though.

So off to the ICU I go. They gave me some real good pain killers there, because it didn't take very long before I was out cold and well into LA LA land. I thank God for that time of no consciousness of pain. Burns have got to be one of the worst forms of pain going, and to be conscious of that pain, along with the pain of all my personal losses would have been far too much to bear.

They had me on so much morphine, that I was having some very vivid nightmares, the one that I remember is actually quite funny now, but it really caused me some concern. From what I have learned since, it caused the Nursing Staff even more concerns. Until I was able to tell them what was happening. You see with burn victims, they need to debride all the dead and decaying skin off. This is done in a big jet tub with Nurses very gently using

DECISIONS

scrub brushes. It felt anything but gentle, and let me tell you, this is pain like you do not want to ever know about. The Nursing staff that did this were primarily Asian women, which will explain part of my nightmare as we continue. The Nurses, (who again were Asian), would come and get my bed and move me to the tub room. Where they would strip me and prepare me for my bath, taking all the bandages off that they could before getting me into the tub and then soaking the rest off inside the tub. They would then start to scrub my skin and the pain was unbearable. I remember screaming, and begging them to stop it hurt so much. But my mind, thank God, was not really there. With my LA LA medications, my dream was this. Whenever the Nurses would come in to get me, I was under the impression that they were trying to steal my body. These Asian Nurses were trying to smuggle me out of the Hospital in the spare tire carrier of an Ambulance, (for what I had no idea, but I was sure they were trying to smuggle me out). It must have been one really big Ambulance eh! Sometimes, they would succeed and they would take me off to where this Asian lady would be waiting for me inside this big pool, (the tub). I would have to get up and move into the pool and then she would start to scrub my body. Her voice was so melodic, I couldn't understand what she was saying, but her voice was so soothing. Her soft touch, but none of it could hide the pain that I felt. I don't remember how I kept getting away, but I would wake up and find myself being moved yet again by an Asian Nurse and be looking for ways to escape. If a Caucasian Nurse would come into my room while I was semi conscious, I would grab her and hold on begging her not to let them take me. Several times, they had to call Security to get me to let go of the Nurse. So you see, the Nurses not knowing what was going on in my LA LA brain were terrified to come into my room. When I got a chance to talk to one of the Nurses after being discharged, she thought it was quite a laugh, and could not wait to tell the other Nurses about my funny LA LA land dreams that had them so concerned about what I was doing.

Some really great things happened while I was in intensive care. The first thing that happened was a friend named Jo-Ann who came and stayed at my bedside right after it happened. No one from my family showed up, but Jo-Ann answered GOD's prompting on her heart and was there for me. The Nurses, have since told me that they did not think I would make it through the first night. When Jo-Ann showed up, they did not want to let her in, but she managed to persuade them to allow her into my

DECISIONS

room. I was burnt so bad that she could not recognize me. My face had swollen to larger than the size of a Medicine Ball, completely hiding my ears and any facial features. My hands had swollen as well to where it looked like I had hockey gloves on, and that was without bandages on. In other words, I was a mess. I guess you could kind of say that I was really burnt up over the whole affair. But Jo-Ann, bless her heart was there. She talked to me, and for the first time my pulse started to pick up a bit. The Nurses have told me that they are sure that the only reason I made it through that night was because of Jo-Ann showing up and staying with me and talking to me and holding my burnt unrecognizable body. Thank you Jo-Ann, from the bottom of my heart, Thank you!

The fourth day that I was in intensive care, my wife served me with Divorce papers. That made it one year exactly from the accident at the Dentist. Because of my condition, they could not serve me, so they had to leave. What a blessing from GOD that was. That same day, my Dad, who I had not seen in 26 years came to my bedside and stayed with me until I was released from intensive care, some 19 days later. All I remember of this time was this withered old man, in this yellow gown and face mask, peering past the Nurses and asking me if I knew who he was. I kept saying no, and he would reply, "I'm your Dad." Boom, I would pass out. What courage my Dad showed me by being there for me! I will always be thankful for that. **Thank you Dad!**

Chapter Five

Suicide Statistics

American Statistics:

—   30,000 Americans commit suicide annually –
    that's 82 people each day - more than 3 each
    hour.

—   Suicide is the eighth leading cause of death in America.

—   About 73 percent of teenagers have thought about committing suicide. Of these, 27 percent have actually tried. **<u>One</u> out of every 5 teenagers has attempted suicide!**

—   Seven out of 10 know someone who has attempted suicide.

Canadian Statistics:

—   From 1979 to 1993, 6,187 persons died from AIDS in Canada, while there were 52,825 suicide deaths.

—   Canada's five year average suicide rate of 12.8 per 100,000 is slightly higher than the average rate of 12.2 per 100,000 in the United States (1989 - 93).

—   12% of all Canadians seriously consider suicide at some time during their life.

—   10 to 13% of suicide attempters ultimately kill themselves.

DECISIONS

—   Males complete suicide more than 3 times as
     often as females. In 1994, 41% of all suicides
     in Canada were males between 15 and 39
     years of age.

— Rates of non-fatal suicidal behavior are
   greater than suicide rates by as much as 100
   to 1.

—

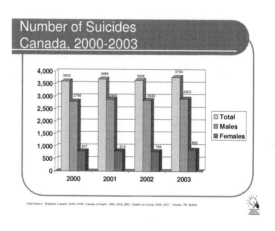

J. K. Proudlock

Chapter Six

Arrested

On day 24, I was discharged from ICU, and moved down to the Burn Ward. Now you have to understand some things here. My wife, via her Policeman friend had gotten the Hospital Staff pretty upset about how I attempted to end my life. That combined with my LA LA trips to the big tub/pool really had some of the Nurses scared about me. So after being in the Burn Ward for only 4 days, the Police showed up and arrested me and charged me with Arson for my attempted suicide. Not only that, but only minutes before they arrived, I was served with the divorce papers from my wife. Talk about hitting a real low. Man, I thought I was low when I attempted suicide, but on that day, I went even lower. The pit of Hell opened up and I was swallowed whole. I was in absolute total shock. My wife did not want me to ever see her or my daughter again, the Police were arresting me, this was it, and I was going to Hell for sure. What a feeling of total despair. There was a total lack of everything that was of any comfort to me. No friends present, no family, no wife, no Church, oh, and yes what about GOD? Where was He? Once again He had failed me. Or so I felt in my anger and shame of that moment.

I guess this is where they talk about adding insult to injury. Arrested and charged with arson for attempting to kill myself. The scales of justice sometimes just don't seem very fair. But fair or not, terror became my Ali. Having never been in jail before, the humiliation of sitting in jail while they took my picture, finger printed me and everything else was very traumatic. Add to that the intense pain of the burns and feeling cold and thirsty, with no loving hand of a Nurse to hold me or get me that extra blanket I so desperately needed to keep

DECISIONS

warm. I was in my own little Hell. I had no one to advise me as to what to do except the Policeman who arrested me. Let me tell you, if you are ever, (and I pray to God that you are never in this situation); **NEVER** take the word of the arresting officer. His advice cost me more than I care to ever remember. Let's just leave it with, don't ever get into a situation where you need to find out about Police, Jail, Lawyers, Judges, Crown Prosecutors, and especially **bad advice**.

After they had processed all the paper etc., they transported me to the Remand Centre, more humiliation. Here I learned that you have to strip in front of everyone and shower and then while naked, stand in front of more people and have them get clothes to fit you; unless of course you are someone like me who has attempted suicide. Because then you get to wear things called "Baby Dolls". These are not the cute little things that women look great in. Instead they are two padded blankets sown together with holes cut out for your head and arms. Not so cute looking, and not very comfortable either. Two very big problems were encountered here. First, the showers are very high pressure designed to take the skin off a normal person at 40 feet, never mind me. Here I am with burns to most of my body and the shower peeled most of the burnt but healing skin right off my body. There I was in intense pain and bleeding all over the place, with no one to help me or to come to my aid. Not a great place to be. After fixing myself up as best I could with burnt torn and bleeding hands, I was left standing in front of the man to get my Baby Dolls. The problem being that because of my burns, I could not get them on. So guess what? They paraded me buck naked down the halls of the Remand Centre past General Population, (which I might add is co-ed), to the OB Ward, (Observation Ward). Humiliation is such an under rated word, but it is the only word we have that I can use to try and explain the feeling of total loss of self; which is what I felt as I hung my head in shame and cried silent dry tears of humiliation.

The OB Ward cells are made so that there is nothing that someone could use in an attempted suicide. They also have cameras that are on all the time and even if you have to go to the bathroom, they watch you. There is no where to hide. My first night in OB was Hell. When you are burnt, your body looses heat like crazy. So there I was buck naked with one very poor blanket and a pillow on a metal bed, with a camera watching my every move. I kept calling the guards and asking for another blanket and no one responded. A person in the OB

DECISIONS

cell next to me was screaming all night and so sleep was a distant thing not to be found that night.

The next morning breakfast was served via a slot in the door and I had to try and carry the tray over to my bed. It was then that I discovered that my cell had not been cleaned before I arrived. There was food scrapes all over the floor and urine all over the floor and toilet, just what I needed with open burns. I guess they never heard the expression of cleanliness is next to Godliness. I felt really scared after seeing what kind of a mess I was in. I was so afraid that I would get infected from all the unclean things that were around.

Next came the morning shower. Terror of terrors. You see the first few minutes after the shower comes on it is freezing cold, and then there is the force of the shower. I didn't know what to say. I was terrified; I didn't want a repeat performance of the night before when I was first brought into the Remand Centre. But, GOD intervened and the guard that helped me that morning was so kind. He not only started the shower at the risk getting wet, but he tied a face cloth across the shower head so that the water just kind of poured out very gently. Not all of the guards/policemen are as bad as we like to make them out to be. Although I did run into my fair share of the bad ones, I was also blessed with some good ones; this was one of the good ones! After my shower, the guard even went as far as trying to help me dry off and then helped me put the towel around me, so that I could walk back to my cell with some dignity. What kindness, thank you my friend who ever you are.

When I got back to my cell, the Nursing staff was there to help me put on my burn garments. What a relief, after fighting so hard the night before to do it all by myself, this was a pleasant and welcome surprise. Then the walk down the hall to wait in the front while they got everyone ready who had a court appearance that day. When they transport prisoners, they put leg shackles and hand cuffs on everyone. The guards were so kind; they saw my burnt hands and left the hand cuffs off. They even helped me get on and off of the bus. Not something that they did for just everyone.

Finally court, this is where the nice arresting Policeman had told me to just go in front of the Judge and take whatever they did to me. I am glad that I was prompted in my heart to speak to not only the Duty Council, but the Doctor they had on duty. The Doctor recommended that I be admitted to the General Hospital for treatment and

DECISIONS

Diagnosis. They also do this to see if a person, like me in this case is fit to stand trial. The 30 day assessment period was very beneficial not only health wise, but also emotionally. The care I got there was bar none the best I had received during my illness and subsequent suicide attempt.

J. K. Proudlock

Chapter Seven

Forensic Unit

This part of the book I dedicate to the Nursing Staff at the Forensic Department of the General Hospital. This ward is an extension of the prison system and all who work there has a job that is difficult at best. I owe all of you more than I could ever repay. You started my healing, whether you may feel this way or not, I looked on you as Angels sent from God to talk to, listen, guide, and nurture me back to physical and emotional health. Lana and Bernie were two Nurses in particular who were charged with my care, and did such a fine job.

Lana, was so beautiful and caring, she knew that the shower was too harsh for me, so she proposed that I use the bathtub. After seeing the extent of my burns and seeing my limited mobility, because I could not get into the tub, let alone move the cloth and soap to bath myself, she even offered to bath me She was so kind and always so concerned about me, and maintaining my dignity, as much as humanly possible in these circumstances. Thank you Lana, your love healed more of my broken heart than you will ever know.

Bernie had a smile that used to light up my day and night depending on the shift she was on. She went well out of her way to help me. She could see the intense pain that I was in and that I was trying to martyr myself by denying myself the medicine that would help me recover both mentally and physically. So she took it on herself to get me more powerful pain medicine. Thank you Bernie, you will always have a special place in my heart.

God really let me open up and spill my heart to

DECISIONS

these two Angels. Not only was I trying to get my physical and emotional health back on track during this time, but I was trying to deal with a divorce and a criminal charge of arson; never mind the ever present reality of past issues that had plagued me most of my life that seemed all too real at the time. Plus having my family, with the exception of my Dad, and most of my friends desert me, it was sure lonely in my little Hell! My friend Jo-Ann, and Garth, were my only contacts.

My wife, who I assume was dealing with her pain in her own way, was draining our joint bank account as soon as my disability cheques would come in. So I could not get money out to hire any lawyers. The bank would not do anything unless I went to them and signed some papers; which was not very possible in my situation. So my friend Garth put up the money for my criminal lawyer, and bail to get me out when the time came. So, as you can see my plate was rather full trying to deal with all the parts of my life that were going down the tubes and that plate seemed to be getting fuller instead of getting emptier.

I credit Lana and Bernie with keeping me focused on what needed to be done with out getting the water too muddy with all the things at once. It didn't matter what time of day or night, or what Nursing staff was on, someone was always ready to talk and to lend an ear. They were so great in helping me change my bandages and making sure that I followed through with my exercises to try and get my hands so that they would function again.

One day after getting some information from both my divorce lawyer and criminal lawyer as to what my wife was doing and saying on the outside I became so angry. My wife had decided during my stay in the General Hospital to speed up the divorce and put it through on 30 days mental cruelty, because of my attempted suicide, and my scene that I caused at the house the night she moved out. I lost it. The nursing staff watched as I put the boxing gloves on and hit the punching bag they had for clients to take out their frustrations on. In absolute pain, I hit the bag. I had no strength, and that was lucky for me, because even with the strength I had, I torn my hands all to pieces doing what I did. When I was done taking my frustration out, with tears pouring down my cheeks, they took me into the medical room and cleaned me all up and listened to me pour out my heart. Not once did they ever give up on me. I was a person with problems, who was earnestly seeking help and understanding. Not someone or some thing that deserved to be left

DECISIONS

alone to die, like some people in my life felt at the time and for that matter, some still do. Because of their decisions they have missed witnessing the awesome healing power of GOD and his Angels of mercy. Angels that He sent my way at times that I needed them the most. Thank you GOD ! ! !

One time while changing my burn garments, one of the Nurses, who had lovely long nails, had her wonderfully fitted, HA HA, latex gloves on and caught the back of my hand with her nail and peeled a section of meat off the back of my hand about 2 inches long, about a 1/4 inch deep and the width of her nail. **PAIN** . . . she felt so bad and tears were pouring down her face as she tried so hard to fix up my hand that she had just innocently damaged. All the while in total disbelief that I was trying to console her, and tell her it was all right. She didn't mean to do it, it was an accident. But she felt so bad, I think I felt just as bad as she did knowing what it was doing to her inside, knowing that she was the cause of my pain. If you read this, you know who you are, and you need to know that I forgive you for the momentary pain you caused me. The love you showed me before and after that little bit of pain has more than made up for it. I owe you a debt of gratitude my true friend.

I guess the two things that I will always remember most about my care here will be my special bath time with Lana. She was always so full of grace and love and never once making me feel ugly because of my burnt condition; always treating me with dignity and respect, but most of all an understanding of my humility in all situations. Thank you Lana, your love and kindness will be a part of me always. Then there was Bernie, Bernie was always full of smiles and humour. She could see how I hid my pain by using humour and trying to make everyone else feel better. Thank you for knowing how much pain I was in and making it your goal to get the medication that I needed. You have a heart that I will always hold dear, thank you!

The Forensic Unit has something called group meetings where everyone is requested to attend. During the meetings, the clients get to talk about what was on their minds as well as sign up for duties like getting coffee ready for snack time, setting up weekly tournaments like pool, crib and bingo etc. The first week I was there, I did not do very much except light duty things, but some how I got the respect of almost all the clients and for the next 3 weeks, I was elected to the Chairpersons position for the group and even that helped in my healing. I was not as useless as everyone on the

DECISIONS

outside had made me feel. Yes, I had, and was still having some difficulties, but I was far from being the person that a lot of people had placed me as; mentally not able to function as a normal human being. Hence, I was not worth listening to and my pain and hurts really didn't matter because, mentally I wasn't all there. **WRONG ! ! !**   I still felt all the same feelings; and my pain and hurts were just as real as the next persons. But the perception is, if you are not all there, you don't feel and you just don't count. Your life is not important.

I wish I could take everyone who was involved in my life during my mental turmoil and let them live in my shoes for just one week of my personal journey through Hell. I really believe it would open their eyes to not only my situation, but to all the thousands of people out there who are genuinely suffering from mental disabilities. My heart pours out to each and every one of them after my own walk in their shoes. When you are having difficulties with your mental status, you need people to gather around you in loving support, not in ridicule and judgement. Our pain is just as real as yours, even more so because it is so intensified in our unbalanced state. But if you, we, me, gather around and love, support, nurture, open up our hearts and lives, we, with GOD's love can restore a broken life. What a joy!

Chapter Eight

Questions

So, the question arises through all this, what about suicide, is it still an option? Or was it ever really an option? Was it even something that I had control over? Even with all the things that were piling up and I do mean piling up, suicide **was not** and **should not** have been an option.

Just because I felt lower than low and that all my so called friends and loved ones were leaving me behind should not have led me to attempting suicide. Suicide has been highlighted by the media as a way out. It is time for us to say NO MORE!!! Suicide needs to be looked at in a way that we can see the damage it leaves behind. Prevention, education are some answers, but a return to biblical family values in my opinion is what needs to happen for any real change to occur. Only when we know who we are in Christ can we fight from a position of strength.

The new medications that they had me on were working to settle me down. They at least were not leaving me feeling right on the edge of being totally out of control, which is where I had been for far too long. The Nursing staff was also very good at being there when I needed someone to talk to and provided many helpful insights as to what may have happened to get me to where I was. The second question, "was suicide ever an option?", though is more difficult to answer. When you feel like you have been through all the hoops, medically and you have faithfully attended all the counselling sessions you have been scheduled for and no one seemed to listen, or believe what you were saying. When you

DECISIONS

have been abandoned by Pastors, family and friends and you feel like even God has forgotten about you. You come to a point of total despair. Even if you have never and I mean *NEVER* thought of suicide in your life before. Suicide looks like the only way out.

! ! ! BUT STOP ! ! !

<u>Please</u>, please don't go there!

Just when things look like the absolute darkest is when the sun/SON is about to shine on you. If you go to where I was and happen to succeed, you will miss the sun/SON. What a shame! Life can be and is full of ups and downs and you know what I mean about downs don't you! But follow the picture; up down up down up down then back up again. Yup, I hear you, there are times when it isn't just down, it is down, . . .down, . . . down, . . . down and more down. Praise GOD! Look at all the way up you get to go now. UP, . . . UP, . . . UP, . . . UP, and even more UP! But I know how hard it is to think about that when you are down. So I beg you please don't give up on this book right now, because the reason I can give you to always look up is soon to be revealed. Stay tuned and get ready for action my friends. **GOD does care and He loves <u>YOU</u>!**

J. K. Proudlock

Suicide is not the option, and should never be an option ! ! !

Please read on . . .

DECISIONS

Chapter Nine

Back to Jail

So, things are looking like they are heading back up again and guess what, crash and burn time again. You see, after my psychiatric examination and they determine that yes I am okay to stand trial, guess where I have to go? Back to jail. I was very lucky, or should I say, GOD was looking out for me. He was providing His chosen guards who were transporting me during my moves from Jail to the General Hospital and back and forth to the Foothills

Hospital Hand Clinic to monitor the progress of my healing. They became real friendly and even though it was required that I be in leg and hand cuffs, they were gracious and did not make me wear the hand cuffs. They were always ready to help me into the van and upstairs what ever it took to be kind. So my trip back to jail was a lot less stressful than it could have been.

Back at jail, it was the same routine, strip, shower and dress in front of who ever was there. But something happened, it was like God reached down and said, hey this guy has just come from the Hospital and is clean, so he doesn't need to shower. And by the way, help him with getting his clothes off and on. Not only that, don't send him back to the OB ward, with those crazy baby dolls that he can't wear, give him some real loose fitting clothes and send him to the Hospital Ward where it is clean and he can be cared for. Praise GOD, what a relief. All the guards and nurses were so kind to me this time. Nothing had changed, except God was there in a very big way. Thank you GOD, for going before me and preparing my way!

The hospital ward is rather neat, you are locked into your cell, and mine was bright and open with lots of windows. So they could monitor me of course. But it was very nice. They even let me use a bath tub instead of the shower. During specific times of the day, they allowed you to go out into a common area and sit and talk with other inmates. There was one very tall fellow who was in the hospital ward because he was a drug addict and he was coming down from all his drugs. The first few days, they just sleep, because of the drugs that they give them to come down. But when I was there, this fellow was just coming out of his stooper and they allowed him into the common area for the first time. Well, he went bezerk and started throwing things and everyone ran to their rooms until the guards came to subdue him, everyone that is except me. I don't know if I was so afraid of him or if God just gave me peace or perhaps took all my strength to run and just had me sit there. But sit there I did. After what seemed like an eternity, he just came over and sat down beside me and said, "Why aren't you afraid of me?" To which for some unknown reason, I replied, "because I know Jesus and He keeps me safe."

Whoa, where did that come from? Here I was questioning if God and His Son really existed and I was witnessing to this man that Jesus was keeping me safe! Unreal, just totally unreal. I was feeling like God was not real, yet I was witnessing to this man that was coming down from a drug high in jail. When the guards arrived, they could not believe what they were seeing. Here we were, the two of us sitting there talking like long lost friends and the anger this man had was totally gone. When they asked him to go to his room, he went peacefully; little did I know how much this one contact would affect so many relationships even after I left jail. God is so neat!

The next day, I was to go to court and try and get out on bail, I was sitting up at the front and this time, one of the regular guards was off and so the other guard said "okay Kim, lets get your leg shackles on and you can go and wait by the bus." Great I thought, things are off to a good start. So on go the leg shackles and off I headed for the bus, but . . . the other guard did not know the routine, or me, so he freaked when I went to go past him to the bus because he saw that I did not have my hand cuffs on. He reached out and grabbed me and in the process, tore all the new skin off my left arm. Instant pain, tears were streaming down my cheeks and then from out of no where there was this scream. But it wasn't me; it was him, the guard.

All the other inmates that knew about me and had heard about the man on drugs and how I had

DECISIONS

reacted jumped the guard. Even the other guards were pounding on him. But of course, they made it look like they were trying to break up the fight. But they were angry at him for what he had done to me and chose to take it out on him in a way that they could cover up. Before it was all over, a Nurse appeared out of no where and whisked me away to clean me up and fix my bandages, which was all fine and dandy, except that the bus taking us prisoners to court had left by this time, so they transported me to the Court House by van. This was lucky for me, because if I had missed my court day, I would have had to wait in jail until they could fit me in again, and that can take some time, and the last thing I wanted to do was be in jail a minute longer than I needed to be. Trust me, it isn't even a nice place to visit, let alone stay for a night or two or three and especially not a place to spend a good portion of ones life. So don't go there my friends, just trust me on this one!

My hearing came and I looked out into court and there was my friend Garth, he had taken time off work to be there for me. What a friend! More than I can say for my family and of course my wife, who didn't show up. Of course then why would she, since she was divorcing me anyway, right? My Dad had planned on being there, but he was given the wrong date and time for my appearance, so he was quite upset that he missed it. But just knowing his heart was to be there for me was more than enough for me at that time. Thanks Dad!

The judge and my lawyer agreed to the following 4 things that the crown put forward:

1. $500.00 cash bail.
2. Attend the Forensic Assessment Outpatient Services on a weekly basis for 1 year.
3. Have **NO** contact with my wife and daughter.
4. Maintain weekly contact with a Probation Officer, also for 1 year.

The cash bail was hard to raise, as my wife was still emptying our joint account of all funds from my disability checks. Since Garth was there, and he knew my cash situation, he placed bail for me. However since he was not prepared to do this at the time, I wound up going back to jail for another night. I was scared of staying in jail, but in a weird way, I felt comforted as well. You see because of how I had conducted myself with the tall dude, I had become family and felt like no one was going to harm me while I was there, or for that matter after I left jail.

DECISIONS

That night I did some reflecting and I began to realize how much my wife hated me. No contact with her or my daughter. Who was this woman I had been married to? If she was divorcing me in my time of need and placing these kind of restrictions on me, obviously, she was not who I thought I married. She was a bitter vengeful person consumed by hate, because only hate can generate so much distorted emotion. For the first time, I realized she was in worse shape than I was, and I began to feel sorry for her and her twisted mind. Not only her, but all those who had come to her rescue, cough cough. Her twisted friends, both sets of our twisted families, and even some people/friends who called themselves children of GOD, these people were the ones who needed people to feel sorry for them, not me. These were the people who really needed to feel a touch from GOD!

I was beginning to see how little my attempted suicide had done to right the wrongs that I was trying so hard to correct. Instead, I had damaged myself beyond recognition with burns; my left hand was damaged so bad that it was never to be useful again. My family, wife, friends, the Church had left me. I had unpaid bills, and no real means of providing for myself, let alone paying child support, or the $3,200.00 I needed every 6 weeks for another set of burn garments, plus the 2 by 2 and 4 by 4 gauze pads, creams, soaps, plus a place to live, food to eat and more. By the time everything was said and done I needed over $5,000.00/month just to pay the bills.

My attempted suicide that had been engineered to end all my pain both physical and emotional' had left me in worse shape than I was in before my attempt. There was a trail of damaged lives and relationships everywhere. Bad move Kim, real bad move! I am beginning to understand at this point the complete lies of what suicide says it will do for you. I can just begin to see how the devil has perverted all the facts and perceived facts to fit in his plan of ultimate destruction.

Suicide:
- It lies when it says it will be your friend and fix every thing if you just go ahead and do it!
- It lies when it says I will end all your pain and the pain of those around you.
- It lies when it says I will end your pain and give pain to those who have done you wrong.

DECISIONS

SUICIDE JUST OUT AND OUT

LIES ABOUT EVERYTHING!

J. K. Proudlock

Chapter Ten

The Booth Center

On October 12th, 1995, just 56 days after my attempted suicide, I was released from jail and found myself with no where to go. So, the Salvation Army Booth Centre in Calgary Alberta, a hostel for men became my home for the next 2 years. My 56 days post attempted suicide broke down to 23 days in intensive care, followed by 4 days in the burn unit and then a total of 29 days in the jail system. This may sound silly, but if I had been able to find a way to stop my wife from draining our joint account of my disability pension from the City, while I was still in jail, I would have stayed in for another 30 days, and possibly even longer had I been able do this one small thing. I knew that I was not in any way shape or form physically or emotionally well enough to be out on my own. Tending to my burns, and trying to maintain my very unstable emotional health, was a huge stretch and it put my health and well being in further jeopardy by insisting on being released far too soon; so that I could put a stop to my checks being taken by my wife. Don't get me totally wrong here; I understand to a point what my wife was doing, she was scared and looking out for number 1. We all do that when we are in crisis mode, but I believe that a lot of her fears were being driven by good meaning friends and family. But once again that is only speculation on my part.

The first hurdle of posting bail was looked after now it was the next one, where was I going to live? Well, thank God for the Salvation Army is all I can say. They have an awesome prison ministry and they found out about my situation and showed up with clothes for me to wear and a place to hang my hat; except at that time I didn't even have a hat to hang up. You see when my wife left she took everything, clothes, underwear even, and the boys that moved

DECISIONS

her out even used my leather coat as a traction matt for the truck that got stuck in the driveway. So here I was at the Booth Center with nothing. I remember feeling so alone, but I had been there before, my past was coming back in waves as I sat on my cot with no where to go and nothing I could do anyway due to my physical condition.

The 4th day that I was there was the start of a new life for me. I walked up to the front check in counter and asked Dan the fellow behind the counter to get my medications for me. They lock all those things up to prevent us street people from selling them or over dosing ourselves while staying there. So, Dan started out by getting all the bottles with my name out on the counter. Then he proceeded to start counting the number of pills each bottle said I was to take. Then I interrupted him and said, "Dan, if God is going to heal me, then He is going to heal me without all these drugs, because these drugs are what made me go to where I went and I am never going back there!" I turned and walked back to my little cot on the main floor and for the 2nd time in my Christian life I prayed to God about me; and He answered.

"God" I said, "Why did you not answer my prayer when I called out to you the night I attempted

Suicide?" His answer was without hesitation and in such a calming and loving voice. "I did" He said. "I sent my Son Jesus Christ to die on the cross for you". For the first time in my Christian life I truly felt the love of Jesus just for me, and I started to cry and my body shook and the reality of what I had just heard started to sink in. Then, God's voice came again. "But that was not enough for you, I was in the truck with you, I pulled you out of the burning fire. It is my hand print on your right hand that no one can explain." This statement of fact almost stopped my breathing as I pulled back the burn garments and looked at the only place on my arm that was not burnt. I could see where the thumb of God had been and where the fingers were wrapped around my arm. At that point the love of God just surrounded me and I accepted answers to many questions I had from my childhood on. All the Whys and where are you, seemed to be answered in that time of quietness with God.

OOPS! Let's not forget where I was when this was all going on. I was on the main floor of the Booth center where there is a whopping 18 inches of space on each side of the cots where men were gathered getting ready to get up for the day and get on with there lives as street people. Try and envision what would happen if a group of men were standing around and one of them a perfect stranger in burn garments started to audibly cry. Yup, you saw things right the whole room cleared in a matter of seconds. Some knew I had attempted suicide and so were running out shouting "He is crazy, he is going to do it again." Others were running out just because as guys we do not know how to deal with emotions shown by others. Trying to figure out a crying woman is tough enough but a crying man is like get out of here it may be contagious! Whatever was going on in each persons head is hard to say, but I can tell you the room cleared faster than if someone had yelled, FIRE!

With all the commotion, the Pastor Les Cross, who liked to sign his name as "- +" showed up and came in to be with me. After hearing what I had to say, Les also broke into tears and we thanked God for His mercy. This began a long friendship where Les would sit in my room and cry as he watched me knit scarves for the 5 people who stayed near me during my recovery. Each stitch was done with so much pain. Each stitch had to be perfect to reflect the love I had for each of these people who in my eyes were hero's for staying close to me when everyone else had given up on me. Each stitch was one more stitch closer to where I so longed to be, in the arms of my wife.

J. K. Proudlock

Chapter Eleven

Where am I Today and how I got here?

Today I sit in front of my computer and ponder at all that I would have missed out on, if I had been successful in my attempted suicide. I am now 54 years old, remarried and then remarried again. This time with a lovely wife, a 9 year old son, a 7 year old daughter, a 1 year old son, and another baby on the way. This is my at home family. I also have 2 daughters that do not live with us and I still hope and pray a time will come when we can get to know each other.

I have done a lot of reading, and have learned to be very careful with whom I choose to hang with. I have also learned to work on keeping my thoughts in control; after all it was my thoughts that led me to attempt to take my life. I look for gems that can keep my day going when all things around me seem to be crashing. Little short ones like this, "Problems are capable of solutions; mysteries have no solutions." Norman R. Depuy

This one I do not know where it came from, "Inch by inch, life's a cinch, yard by yard life is hard. Do you get what I am trying to say here? If we look at all we have to do, and all the things we have done wrong, and all the things people expect from us; life looks so hard. So break it down and look at things inch by inch. When I started getting my life back together I became overwhelmed several times and it was little quotes just like this one that made me sit back and realize what I was doing wrong. I remember many times as a kid my Dad saying life is as hard as you want to make it. Why did it take me so long to hear the meaning of those words?

DECISIONS

I spend a lot more time in prayer now than I ever did before. Prayer doesn't have to be hard either. I call out to my friend who never leaves me and seek council on all aspects of my life. Before I actually tried to put God in a box and tell Him what areas of my life He could have control of. I've been learning to ease up a bit and give more of my life over to God so He can teach me His ways and I can learn from Him.

Through prayer and looking inside myself I discovered a lot of what I will label emotional baggage. I had a lot of broken relationships, within my family, friends and more. I was holding onto a lot of things, emotions, feelings. Some of these feelings were justified and others were just plain old B.S. The Bible speaks about forgiveness and I let it slide by saying to myself, "But I am right in feeling the way I do." Then I read a little quote that opened my eyes all the way. "Forgiveness is the key that unlocks the handcuffs of hate." William Ward is the author of that one and what he said in those few words finally showed me that until I forgave all the people who had wronged me, I would continue to get the same things I had always gotten. I needed to fix me!

By holding onto the emotions of past hurts I was

doomed to follow the same path over and over. How could I have missed this powerful truth for so many years? Once I learned to let go, I found the woman of my dreams, one with the strength of character to stick by me in the dark times, one who loves me no matter what happens and is there to pick up the pieces with me and start over as we have had to do several times in our brief time together. No bickering over small things, no holding onto every little wrong done and then bringing it out to taunt, inflame and wreck the peace that floods our home. Male or female our tongue can wreck the peace of our home and we need to guard that sanctuary with all the skills that we possess.

I have also learned that as a man I need to have what I call life lines open and ready to use. I keep myself grounded by staying on top of these nasty little things that keep arriving at our doorstep. Broken water pumps for the well, broken windows, flat tires, speeding tickets, and more, things that for the most part are just a regular part of life, but to someone who has been depressed, or on the verge of depression it can be the single one thing that sets us over the edge. So my life lines are a group of what I call my true friends, top of my list is my wife, then an old friend in Calgary, a new friend who lives close by and a neighbor who has

DECISIONS

been in a very similar place that I was.

I also have my family back in my life now, my sister next to me in lineage, and my older brother. My Dad past away not long ago and I am sad to say that we once again were not speaking when that happened: my Mom past away several years before my Dad and I missed out on reconnecting with her as well. My oldest sister is still a pain, but God has given me peace about her so I just let her be her and keep my distance as much as possible. My step-mom, who at this time has become my Mom, has proven to be a woman of faith and strength of character that has blessed our lives over and over again. These are my life lines! Your life line may be very different than mine, but it needs to be there and it needs to be cultivated, weeded regularly, and feed a lot more wholesome food than just plain old guy B.S. Us guys especially need to break down the walls of silence and open up and share the burden of those around us, and speak out about the pain that holds us captive. Only once that is accomplished can we make serious strides in healing this awful tragedy of a life lost to suicide.

I have also reduced my risk behavior. What does that mean? Well, I have slowed down my life, learned to have and to make time for my family. Slowed down my driving, stopped climbing towers, no more satellite installs on the peak of a 12/12 pitch roof over looking a 250 foot drop into the great abyss. No more sitting at the computer until all hours of the night, my family has become the most important thing on earth for me to look after.

OOPS! There is one other person who is more important to me than my family and that is me. I have learned that if I do not look after myself then I can not be here for them. So I have learned to listen to advice I gave out far too often for others and never took it for myself. I am putting my oxygen mask on; so that I can be here for years to come and see my family grow up and try each day to improve over the day before.

I have also learned not to base who I am on what others think of me or what they think I should be doing, or for that matter not doing. For far too long I listened to what everyone else thought about me, along with everyone around me; that I found myself continually changing to meet the expectations of these friends; these critics. I never really found out who I was, and for that matter, it didn't really matter either. Or so I thought!

So I do a lot more filtering than I ever did before, if what I hear fits with what I believe I am trying

DECISIONS

to become, I let it sink in. If it is contrary to what I believe myself to be, then I discard it and carry on. I let myself be more vulnerable now, and that is not a bad thing. We are taught that we have to be self sufficient, that we have to be able as men to take care of our family. Be the provider, don't show emotion, BUCK UP, cowboy up, and so much more. When we feel vulnerable we run around and get nothing accomplished, except get our blood pressure up. This is when we need to have a friend, a good friend who will listen.

Listen up here to this little ditty I am about to expound on:

REAL MEN, REAL WOMEN, just plain real people, show their strength when they show that they value themselves enough to ask for support. They do not criticize themselves when they need support. They recognize their human needs and take care of them!

My life is so much richer now that I have cast off all the old feelings of low to no self worth. I take time to even stop the van while I am on the road to take in a moment of enjoying all the wonders around me.

Some of us are like a bottle of prescription drugs

with a label on that says "Shake well before using",
I truly hope and pray that you can take some of the
shaking that I went through and use it wisely in
your life, so you don't even think of going where I
went on August 18th, 1995.

Chapter Twelve

Scripture References that may help

Matthew 11:28 – 30

"Come to me, all you who are weary and burdened, and I will give you rest. Take my yoke upon you and learn from me, for I am gentle and humble in heart, and you will find rest for your souls. For my yoke is easy and my burden is light."

Jer. 31:3-4

"The Lord appeared to us in the past, saying:
"I have loved you with an everlasting love;
I have drawn you with loving-kindness.
I will build you up again
and you will be rebuilt, O Virgin Israel.
Again you will take up your tambourines
and go out to dance with the joyful.""

Jer. 29:11-14

"For I know the plans I have for you," declares the Lord, "Plans to prosper you and not to harm you, plans to give you hope and a future. Then you will call upon me and come to pray to me, and I will listen to you. You will seek me and find me when you seek me with all your heart. I will be found by you," declares the Lord, " and will bring you back from captivity. I will gather you from all the nations and places where I have banished you," declares the Lord, "and will bring you back to the place from which I carried you into exile."
I Cor. 13
The love chapter (The Message)

DECISIONS

1Co 13:1 If I speak with human eloquence and angelic ecstasy but don't love, I'm nothing but the creaking of a rusty gate.

1Co 13:2 If I speak God's Word with power, revealing all his mysteries and making everything plain as day, and if I have faith that says to a mountain, "Jump," and it jumps, but I don't love, I'm nothing.

1Co 13:3 If I give everything I own to the poor and even go to the stake to be burned as a martyr, but I don't love, I've gotten nowhere. So, no matter what I say, what I believe, and what I do, I'm bankrupt without love.

1Co 13:4 Love never gives up. Love cares more for others than for self. Love doesn't want what it doesn't have. Love doesn't strut, Doesn't have a swelled head,

1Co 13:5 Doesn't force itself on others, Isn't always "me first," Doesn't fly off the handle, Doesn't keep score of the sins of others,

1Co 13:6 Doesn't revel when others grovel, Takes pleasure in the flowering of truth,

1Co 13:7 Puts up with anything, Trusts God always, Always looks for the best, Never looks back, But keeps going to the end.

1Co 13:8 Love never dies. Inspired speech will be over some day; praying in tongues will end; understanding will reach its limit.

1Co 13:9 We know only a portion of the truth, and what we say about God is always incomplete.

1Co 13:10 But when the Complete arrives, our incompletes will be cancelled.

1Co 13:11 When I was an infant at my mother's breast, I gurgled and cooed like any infant. When I grew up, I left those infant ways for good.

1Co 13:12 We don't yet see things clearly. We're squinting in a fog, peering through a mist. But it won't be long before the weather clears and the sun shines bright! We'll see it all then, see it all as clearly as God sees us, knowing him directly just as he knows us!

1Co 13:13 But for right now, until that completeness, we have three things to do to lead us toward that consummation: Trust steadily in God, hope unswervingly, love extravagantly. And the best of the three is love.

Psalms 32:1-5

"Blessed is he
whose transgressions are forgiven,
whose sins are covered.
Blessed is the man
whose sin the Lord does not count against him

DECISIONS

and in whose spirit is no deceit.

When I kept silent,
my bones wasted away
through my groaning all day long.
For day and night
your hand was heavy upon me;
my strength was sapped
as in the heat of summer.
Then I acknowledged my sin to you
and did not cover up my iniquity.
I said, "I will confess
my transgressions to the Lord" -
and you forgave
the guilt of my sin."

J. K. Proudlock

Chapter Thirteen

Closing Remarks

Praise God! So where are you now on the subject of suicide? Does it still call out to you? Does it keep you awake at night, haunt you day and night? Then turn to God my friend, God and his son Jesus Christ are the only thing that will be there for you no matter what. God is awesome, but there are many times when we need to see the image of Christ with skin on. This is where the life lines that I spoke about come into play, we need to see that human face looking back at us or hear that voice of calmness on the end of the phone line. We do not need answers; we need the validation that we count that we matter and that our feelings while they may not be correct are heard at that moment in time. We need that place of safety, and most of all we need to understand at all times that we do not need to act upon all our feelings. In many circumstances it is better to sleep on them than to act immediately.

Suicide, are you still repulsed? Good, stay there! But do you see the other side? Are you willing to help a friend in need, without putting them down for being down? If not, then I urge you also to turn to God, for only God can give you true understanding of this awful, scary thing.

SUICIDE, don't let it be you!

Religion may not be the answer you have wanted to find by reading my book. You may have been looking for answers to all your questions, all the WHYS, the HOW COMES, the WHY ME'S, and more. No one can give you answers to those questions here on earth. You can seek counseling, and for many that is

DECISIONS

the answer they need for now. Others may just take time to heal and mend wounds created by the parting of someone close, but don't forget to be open to talking to someone about how you are feeling while you deal with your inner turmoil. Don't let the silence engulf you, seek answers and help. The next Chapter will list some references where to go for help.

I pray this has helped even one person in their struggle to become whole.

Regarding people who have been mentioned in this story; all of us need to realize that when a struggle hits we will not always act correctly, or for that matter appropriately. I have chosen to forgive those who did not act appropriately during my ordeal and I ask each of them to forgive me for the same. Life can deal us some things that nothing we have in our tool belt can prepare us for, all we can do is our best. That is what I am trying to do now. I hope and pray that message is strong enough and to the point enough for those out there to hear and understand. Thanks for doing your best! I will continue the struggle to do my best as well. Blessings to all.

J. K. Proudlock

Chapter Fourteen

Where to find help?

First things first! Take a deep breath and realize that you are important! There are people out there that care about YOU! There is another answer, and this list is just a starting point of where to look. Please do not stop looking; YOUR life is important if to no one else, it is to me.

Websites that offer Help

www.suicidehelpwestman.com

www.youtube.com/watch?v=n6LRvi0s2uU

www.suicidehelp.ca

Phone numbers

9-1-1

Canada: 1 800 668-6868

(note: this is the kids help phone # only, there is no National phone number in Canada for Suicide Help, Check your local White Page listings for Regional phone numbers or just call 9-1-1, but call!)

DECISIONS

USA: 1 800 621-4000

J. K. Proudlock

Chapter Fifteen

The Last Kick at the Cat

The Golf Ball Story:

Have you ever taken a golf ball apart? They are pretty wild inside aren't they?

Picture the small center core and label it "**Who I am**".

Next picture the bits of rubber inside that look like giant rubber bands all glued together, this is the middle layer, and label it; "**What I can do**".

Finally picture the hard outer shell, label this part "**What I have**"

The two outer circles represent the way you present yourself to those around you.

What I have, my accumulated treasures and possessions is readily seen by all. Some possessions I was born with: looks, brains, (and sometimes that is more apparent than others), talents, and capabilities. Some treasures I have constructed myself, my job, house, car, furniture and then there was the biggy for me, the size and power of my stereo. Some of us may have children, a marriage, or significant other as treasures.

When the superficial hard outer shell is peeled away, others will soon discover, "What I can do". Some of what I can do will be dictated by "What I have"; such as my capabilities. The remainder of "What I can do" is the result of how I choose to use my abilities. You can see how well I do in

DECISIONS

parenting, maintaining a home, serving my Church, making or saving money, influencing others, and keeping or not keeping my marriage together.

When a gold club hits a golf ball too hard, the ball is split open. If the protective shell is peeled off, the next layer is exposed, and those rubber bands start popping off, and soon you are left with the center core. A crime that you may find more heinous than another, a personal tragedy such as the death of someone close, or as in my case the loss of my identity due to memory loss and marital failure can split you open and begin the process of peeling away your layers of protection.

Once the center core of "Who I am" is exposed, you have options. Our natural tendency might be to try and tape up ourselves, the damaged ball. Add some glue to the mix to keep those rubber bands inside us from popping off, in an effort of keeping our inner core from being exposed.

You can do a patch job, quickly filling your layers of "What I have" and "What I can do", based on a previous set of values. It might even work for awhile, but it is not a very good long term solution. A patch job leaves you damaged, hurting deep inside; unable to fly straight and true when the next golf club of life strikes.

The other choice is to rebuild your life around a new set of values,

If your outer layer has some patch jobs in it; I encourage you to take time now, not tomorrow or next year. But right now to get to know who you are! So; that in dealing with your life, job, family, traffic, or whatever else, you do not find yourself where I found myself.
Take inventory, if we are totally honest with ourselves, we will admit we do have some patch jobs in our outer shell. Some are stronger than others, but they are there none the less. If we base all of "Who we are" on "What I have", or "What I can do", and we loose our possessions or we loose our abilities, or even worse we loose who we are based on the last poll at the local Pub because we offended some ones space at a given moment in time. . . Who are we? . . . Who are you? . . . Who am I?

This is where we need to rebuild "Who we are" on a set of values that does not change. Personally I have found only one person that I can trust and believe in and who believes in me, and that is GOD. No matter where I am or what I have done, His love

DECISIONS

for me never changes. I can make mistakes, leave and turn my back, but He treats me like a long lost friend when I return. What a friend I have in JESUS. He is the rock I have decided to build the new me on. He has begun a work in me that He won't stop until He has finished it. I am far from perfect, but I am so much closer than I have ever been. I pray, my openness in all this has helped open your eyes to possibly your needs or to see the needs of others around you. May God richly bless you as you journey through life, may your days be filled with happiness and joy.